CONTENTS

PART FOUR:
THEMES, CONTEXTS AND SETTINGS

PART FIVE:
FORM, STRUCTURE AND LANGUAGE

PART SIX:
PROGRESS BOOSTER ★

PART SEVEN:
FURTHER STUDY AND ANSWERS

YORK NOTES

The Strange Case of

Dr Jekyll and Mr Hyde

ROBERT LOUIS STEVENSON

NOTES BY ANNE ROONEY

PEARSON

YORK PRESS

The right of Anne Rooney to be identified as Author of this Work
has been asserted by her in accordance with the Copyright,
Designs and Patents Act 1988

YORK PRESS
322 Old Brompton Road, London SW5 9JH

PEARSON EDUCATION LIMITED
Edinburgh Gate, Harlow,
Essex CM20 2JE, United Kingdom

Associated companies, branches and representatives throughout the world

First published 2015

10 9 8 7 6 5

ISBN 978–1–4479–8218–0

Illustrations by Jeff Anderson; and Rob Foote (page 61 only)
Phototypeset by DTP Media
Printed in Slovakia

Photo credits: frotos/Shutterstock for page 12 top / Science photo/Shutterstock
for page 14 middle / Ruddy Bagozi/Shutterstock for page 19 top / Konstantin
Tronin/Shutterstock for page 21 middle / Shaiith/Shutterstock for page 22
bottom / MOSO IMAGE/Shutterstock for page 24 bottom / nobeastsofierce/
Shutterstock for page 25 bottom / Ricardo Reitmeyer/Shutterstock for page 27
middle / Constantine Pankin/Shutterstock for page 30 top / LiAndStudio/
Shutterstock for page 31 top / Willequet Manuel/Shutterstock for page 33
bottom / © iStock/ ©221A for page 34 middle / Sumire8/Shutterstock for page
35 top / De santis paolo/Thinkstock for page 37 middle / auremar/Shutterstock
for page 39 bottom / Tony Bowler/Shutterstock for page 40 bottom /
hanhanpeggy/Thinkstock for page 41 middle / Christian Chan/Shutterstock for
page 42 bottom / LUNAMARINA/Thinkstock for page 43 bottom / Matthew
Jacques/Shutterstock for page 44 bottom / Pete Spiro/Shutterstock for page 45
bottom / Studio-Annika/Thinkstock for page 46 bottom / Volt Collection/
Thinkstock for page 47 bottom / Steve Allen/Shutterstock for page 50 bottom /
Micael Nussbaumer/Shutterstock for page 56 bottom / Pictoral Press Ltd/Alamy
for page 57 top / Lightspring/Shutterstock for page 58 bottom / PeterPaunchey/
Thinkstock for page 59 bottom / Tanchic/Shutterstock for page 63 middle /
Jupiterimages/Thinkstock for page 65 bottom / Holly Kuchera/Shutterstock for
page 66 bottom / withGod/Shutterstock for page 68 bottom / wavebreakmedia/
Shutterstock for page 77 middle

PART ONE: GETTING STARTED

PREPARING FOR ASSESSMENT

HOW WILL I BE ASSESSED ON MY WORK ON *THE STRANGE CASE OF DR JEKYLL AND MR HYDE*?

All exam boards are different but whichever course you are following, your work will be examined through these four Assessment Objectives:

Assessment Objectives	Wording	Worth thinking about ...
AO1	Read, understand and respond to texts. Students should be able to: • maintain a critical style and develop an informed personal response • use textual references, including quotations, to support and illustrate interpretations.	• How well do I know what happens, what people say, do, etc? • What do *I* think about the key ideas in the novella? • How can I support my viewpoint in a really convincing way? • What are the best quotations to use and when should I use them?
AO2	Analyse the language, form and structure used by a writer to create meanings and effects, using relevant subject terminology where appropriate.	• What specific things does the writer 'do'? What choices has Stevenson made? (Why this particular word, phrase or paragraph here? Why does this event happen at this point?) • What effects do these choices create? Suspense? Ironic laughter? Reflective mood?
AO3	Show understanding of the relationships between texts and the contexts in which they were written.	• What can I learn about society from the book? (What does it tell me about attitudes to science in Stevenson's day, for example?) • What was society like in Stevenson's time? Can I see it reflected in the story?
AO4 *	Use a range of vocabulary and sentence structures for clarity, purpose and effect, with accurate spelling and punctuation.	• How accurately and clearly do I write? • Are there small errors of grammar, spelling and punctuation I can get rid of?

* AO4 is assessed by OCR only.

Look out for the Assessment Objective labels throughout your York Notes Study Guide – these will help to focus your study and revision!

The text used in this Study Guide is the Penguin English Library edition, 2012.

HOW TO USE YOUR YORK NOTES STUDY GUIDE

You are probably wondering what is the best and most efficient way to use your York Notes Study Guide on *The Strange Case of Dr Jekyll and Mr Hyde*. Here are three possibilities:

A step-by-step study and revision guide	A 'dip-in' support when you need it	A revision guide after you have finished the novella
Step 1: Read Part Two as you read the novella as a companion to help you study it. **Step 2:** When you need to, turn to Parts Three to Five to focus your learning. **Step 3:** Then, when you have finished, use Parts Six and Seven to hone your exam skills, revise and practise for the exam.	Perhaps you know the book quite well, but you want to check your understanding and practise your exam skills? Just look for the section which you think you need most help with and go for it!	You might want to use the Notes after you have finished your study, using Parts Two to Five to check over what you have learned, and then work through Parts Six and Seven in the weeks immediately leading up to your exam.

HOW WILL THE GUIDE HELP YOU STUDY AND REVISE?

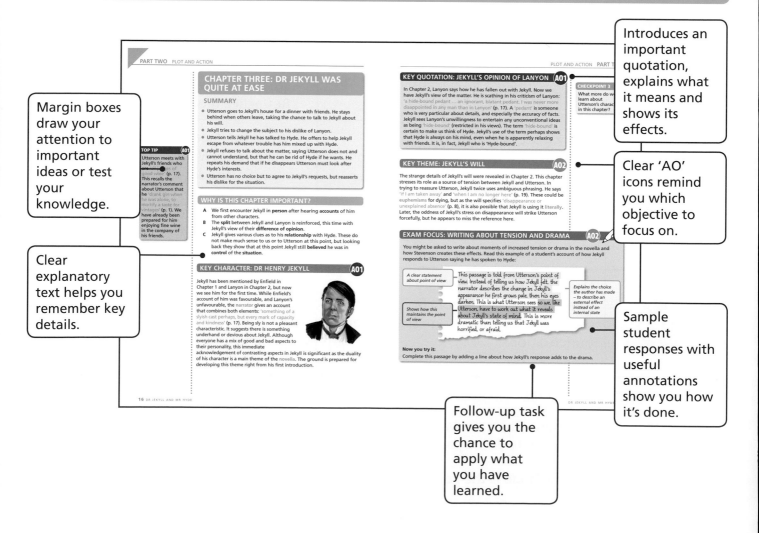

Margin boxes draw your attention to important ideas or test your knowledge.

Clear explanatory text helps you remember key details.

Introduces an important quotation, explains what it means and shows its effects.

Clear 'AO' icons remind you which objective to focus on.

Sample student responses with useful annotations show you how it's done.

Follow-up task gives you the chance to apply what you have learned.

Themes are explained clearly with bullet points which give you ideas you might use in your essay responses.

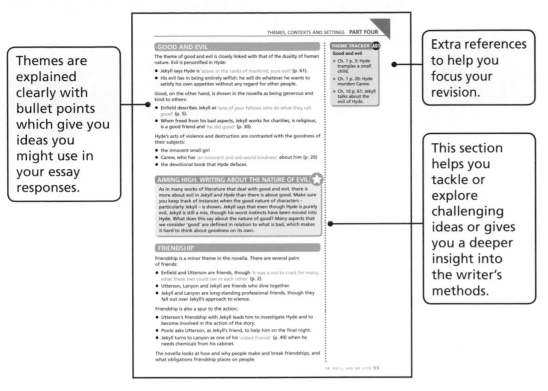

Extra references to help you focus your revision.

This section helps you tackle or explore challenging ideas or gives you a deeper insight into the writer's methods.

Parts **Two** to **Five** end with a **Progress and Revision Check**:

Further substantial and 'open' tasks test your understanding.

A set of quick questions tests your knowledge of the text.

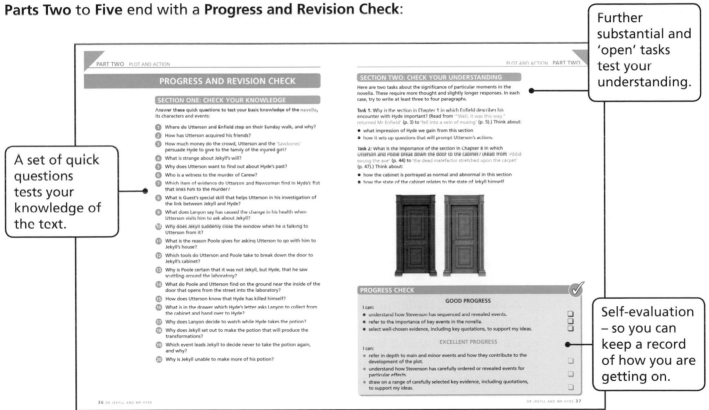

Self-evaluation – so you can keep a record of how you are getting on.

Don't forget **Parts Six** and **Seven**, with advice and practice on **improving your writing skills**:

- Focus on **difficult areas** such as **'context'** and **'inferences'**
- **Short snippets** of **other students' work** to show you how it's done (or not done!)
- Three annotated **sample responses** to a task **at different levels**, with **expert comments**, to help you judge your own level
- **Practice questions**
- **Answers** to the **Progress and Revision Checks** and **Checkpoint** margin boxes

Now it's up to you! Don't forget – there's even more help on our website with more sample answers, essay planners and even online tutorials. Go to www.yorknotes.com to find out more.

PLOT SUMMARY: WHAT HAPPENS IN *THE STRANGE CASE OF DR JEKYLL AND MR HYDE?*

The novella relates events leading up the death of Dr Henry Jekyll, telling some of them two or three times from different points of view. The first version is told by a third-person narrator, who knows little of the inside story. The second version is told by a friend of Jekyll's, Dr Lanyon, and the last is told by Jekyll himself.

CHAPTER 1 – THE DOOR

Mr Utterson, a lawyer, is walking with his friend Mr Enfield when they come to a shabby door. Enfield tells him that he once saw a strangely repellent man called Mr Hyde trample a child and then go through that door to fetch money to pay off the girl's family.

CHAPTER 2 – THE SEARCH FOR HYDE

Utterson looks after Jekyll's will, which leaves all Jekyll's possessions to Hyde in the case of Jekyll's death or disappearance. Disturbed, Utterson visits Lanyon, a colleague and friend of Jekyll. Lanyon has not heard of Hyde, and says he has fallen out with Jekyll. Utterson waits near the door until he manages to see and speak to Hyde. He finds him as unpleasant as Enfield had said he was.

CHAPTER 3 – JEKYLL IS INTRODUCED

Utterson asks Jekyll about Hyde and the will. Jekyll refuses to talk about either, saying the will cannot be changed and he has an interest in Hyde that he will not discuss.

CHAPTER 4 – THE CAREW MURDER

A year later, Hyde murders a man in the street. The police find a letter addressed to Utterson on the body. Utterson identifies the body of Sir Danvers Carew and leads the police to Hyde's home, but he is not in. Looking in his rooms, they find evidence of a hurried departure and half of the walking stick used to kill Carew.

CHAPTER 5 – JEKYLL IS ILL

Utterson visits Jekyll and finds him sick and distraught. He assures Utterson he will never see Hyde again, and shows him a letter apparently from Hyde saying he can escape. Utterson shows the letter to Mr Guest, who is a handwriting expert. Comparing it with a note from Jekyll, Guest notices that the two samples of writing are very similar.

CHECKPOINT 1 (A02)

Which aspects of Utterson's character set out in the first chapter lead us to trust his point of view?

CHAPTER 6 – LANYON DIES

Utterson dines with Jekyll and Lanyon, but a few days later Jekyll will not see him. Utterson visits Lanyon, but finds him very sick, blaming a terrible shock he has had. Lanyon refuses to discuss Jekyll. A few days later, Lanyon dies. He leaves a letter for Utterson to read if Jekyll dies or disappears.

CHAPTER 7 – JEKYLL AT THE WINDOW

Walking with Enfield again, Utterson sees Jekyll at his window. Jekyll says he is too sick to come out. They agree to talk through the window, but a look of horror crosses Jekyll's face and he slams the window shut.

CHAPTER 8 – HYDE'S SUICIDE

Jekyll's butler, Poole, begs Utterson to go with him to Jekyll's laboratory: he fears Jekyll has been murdered. They break the door down and find Hyde's body on the floor; he has just killed himself by taking poison. They find a new will made out to benefit Utterson, and a long statement from Jekyll, but no sign of Jekyll himself.

CHAPTER 9 – LANYON'S LETTER

This chapter is told in Lanyon's letter. One night, Lanyon had received a strange note from Jekyll begging him to fetch a drawer of chemicals from his laboratory and give it to a man who would visit him at midnight. Lanyon is visited by a small, ugly man (Hyde). The man mixes the chemicals to make a potion, which he drinks. Moments later, he is transformed into Jekyll. The shock is more than Lanyon can stand.

CHAPTER 10 – JEKYLL'S STATEMENT

This chapter takes the form of a statement from Jekyll. He had long felt that he had a dual nature: one hard-working and serious, and the other self-indulgent and pleasure-seeking. His scientific work led him to a way of separating the two. He made a potion which freed the negative part of himself to take its pleasures without incriminating him. Soon, this part grew in strength and indulged in more violent and unpleasant acts. Until the murder of Carew, Jekyll switched between the two identities using the potion. Then he stopped using the potion, but began to change spontaneously, and had to use the potion to change back. Finally, he ran out of one of the chemicals he needed for the potion. After taking the final dose, he wrote his statement for Utterson to read.

TOP TIP (A01)

Poole plays a vital role in giving Utterson an account of Jekyll's behaviour at home, and of the few appearances of Hyde in the area of the laboratory. This is information that Utterson – and so we – could otherwise not have access to.

REVISION FOCUS: MAKE SURE YOU KNOW WHAT HAPPENS

Many events are narrated more than once in *Jekyll and Hyde*, first as part of the main narrative and then by Lanyon or Jekyll. Make sure you know the events in the right sequence, and also know how much is revealed about each important event in the main narrative, Lanyon's letter and Jekyll's statement. Make a chart showing the main events in Jekyll's history over the course of the action, and beside each one note what is revealed in each telling of the episode.

CHAPTER ONE: STORY OF THE DOOR

SUMMARY

- Mr Gabriel Utterson is introduced, taking his usual Sunday walk with his relative, Mr Richard Enfield.
- In a well-kept street, they see a battered door, which prompts Enfield to tell Utterson of a recent experience.
- Late at night, Enfield had seen a short man run into and trample over a small girl. He had shouted to stop the man and raise the alarm.
- The girl was not badly hurt, but the crowd of people who had formed had taken such a dislike to the short man that they pressed him for money for the girl's family. He agreed to give £100.
- The man led the group to the battered door, went inside, and came out with gold and a cheque, signed by a very respectable citizen, whom Enfield doesn't name. This led Enfield to suppose Hyde was blackmailing the person who signed the cheque.
- Utterson asks what type of person the short man was. Enfield says there was something very disturbing about him, but he can't quite say what. The man's name was Mr Hyde.

WHY IS THIS CHAPTER IMPORTANT?

A   It introduces Utterson, from whose point of view we will see much of the **action**.

B   Hyde is introduced through Enfield's narrative. We see him acting **violently**, and everyone finding him **repellent**.

C   We see the **setting** in London, with the dilapidated door that will turn out to be Hyde's usual way into **Jekyll's laboratory**.

TOP TIP **A01**

In *Jekyll and Hyde*, Stevenson uses some phrases which are no longer common, such as 'the very pink of the proprieties' (p. 5) and 'a nut to crack' (p. 2). Make sure you understand their meaning.

KEY CONTEXT **A03**

Enfield says of Hyde mowing down the girl that 'it was like some damned Juggernaut' (p. 3). A Juggernaut was a huge wagon which carried the image of the Hindu god Krishna. Traditionally, worshippers were thought to throw themselves under the wheels of the wagon and be crushed to death. Stevenson uses this image to show the violence and force with which Hyde ran into the child.

KEY CHARACTER: MR GABRIEL JOHN UTTERSON (A01)

Utterson is the voice of reason in the novella. The first chapter is important in starting to establish him as a reliable and rational man whose view of events we can trust. The narrator gives us a full and direct account of Utterson, including what he looks like, his habit of speaking little but acting kindly, and his tolerance of others.

By having the narrator describe Utterson directly, Stevenson makes sure we have a clear idea of him from the start. Writers often reveal characterisation through the acts and speech of the individuals themselves and others around them, but this makes it possible for readers to make mistakes in reading a character. Stevenson's direct approach to Utterson avoids this danger.

Utterson does not sound appealing at first: his appearance is 'rugged', he speaks little and he shows no emotion. Yet as the paragraph progresses, we discover more endearing aspects of him – just as those who meet him encounter first someone who is 'lean, long, dusty, dreary' (p. 1) but then find that he is 'somehow lovable'.

KEY SETTING: THE DOOR TO JEKYLL'S LABORATORY (A02)

Seeing the door prompts Enfield to tell his story. It looks immediately out of place in the street as Enfield and Utterson approach it: it is battered with peeling paint, in a street which is otherwise cheery and attractive, with 'freshly painted shutters, well-polished brasses, and general cleanliness and gaiety' (p. 2). Through Enfield describing the setting to Utterson, Stevenson is able to show it to us.

The door is the first glimpse we get of Jekyll's laboratory. It is a 'sinister block of building' (p. 2) jutting into the street, showing signs of neglect and decay. Tramps slouch around it, showing that no one is taking care of the building or minding how it is used.

This sinister first view of Jekyll's property will seem significant later when we discover that the building, like Jekyll himself, has two contrasting aspects.

KEY THEME: HYDE'S UNNATURALNESS (A02)

Enfield's account of Hyde callously trampling the young girl makes Hyde appear immediately unnatural. This unnaturalness is hinted at again when Enfield says that there was something deeply unpleasant about Hyde but he couldn't say what: 'There is something wrong with his appearance; something displeasing, something downright detestable. I never saw a man I so disliked, and yet I scarce know why' (p. 6). This feeling is shared by other characters; it indicates a subconscious awareness that Hyde is somehow unnaturally evil.

Enfield is not alone in feeling like this about Hyde. He says that the doctor turned 'sick and white with the desire to kill him' (p. 4) and he had to keep the women from attacking Hyde because they were 'as wild as harpies' (p. 4).

KEY CONTEXT (A03)

Victorian readers were more familiar with references to the Bible and classical Greek and Roman literature than many readers are today. When Utterson says 'I incline to Cain's heresy' (p. 1), he is referring to the Bible story of Cain killing his brother, Abel. When God asks where Abel is, Cain answers 'Am I my brother's keeper?' Utterson means that he does not take responsibility for other people.

KEY CONTEXT (A03)

In Greek mythology, harpies were winged monsters with women's faces who avenged wrong-doing.

KEY THEME: MEDICINE (A03)

The doctor who attends the trampled girl is the first medical professional to appear in the novella, but both Lanyon and Jekyll are also medical doctors. The term 'Sawbones' (p. 4) that Enfield uses is slightly disparaging. It comes from a time when doctors could do little to treat sick or injured people and the  type of crude surgery that took place – such as amputating crushed or diseased limbs – was carried out by people with little medical training. They were called 'Sawbones' because they used saws to cut through bones during amputations. Enfield tells us that this doctor spoke with an Edinburgh accent, which suggests he trained at the famous and respected medical school in Edinburgh. This would make him more than a 'Sawbones', so Enfield is showing disdain or lack of respect in using the term. As Stevenson grew up in Edinburgh, he would have been well aware of the good reputation of doctors trained there.

KEY THEME: MAKING MISTAKES (A02)

Enfield calls the house with the door 'Blackmail House' (p. 5) because he assumes the only reason someone like Jekyll would give money to a person like Hyde is that he is being blackmailed. He describes the person who wrote the cheque (Jekyll) as 'the very pink of the proprieties, celebrated too' (p. 5) – meaning someone who is respected and beyond suspicion. Utterson accepts Enfield's assumption and later acts on it. As readers, we take the same view, having no reason to challenge it.

As it turns out, Enfield is wrong about the blackmail. This is the first of many mistakes and wrong assumptions in the course of the novella. They help Stevenson to maintain suspense and surprise.

TOP TIP: WRITING ABOUT ENFIELD (A01)

It's important to be able to write about the way Enfield behaves and interacts with Utterson, the only character we see him with. Enfield seems to be an unlikely friend for Utterson. Enfield is a 'well-known man about town' (p. 2), while Utterson is cold and dry. Although the pair value and look forward to their weekly walks, they talk little and seem relieved if they meet someone else.

What he says reveals more about his character. Enfield doesn't like to ask questions. He says, 'You start a question, and it's like starting a stone. You sit quietly on the top of a hill; and away the stones goes, starting others' (p. 5). This suggests that he prefers to be in control and doesn't like unpredictable consequences.

TOP TIP (A02)

Look carefully at the language Enfield uses to talk about Hyde and his actions. How does he convey his dislike and distrust even when not talking directly about it?

CHAPTER TWO: SEARCH FOR MR HYDE

SUMMARY

- At home, Utterson reads over Dr Jekyll's strange will. It states that if Jekyll dies or disappears, Hyde shall take over his life and possessions.

- Utterson goes to visit a friend, Dr Hastie Lanyon, who knows Jekyll well. Lanyon has not heard of Hyde, but says he no longer speaks to Jekyll as they fell out ten years before when Jekyll developed ideas that Lanyon thought unscientific.

- After troubled dreams, Utterson decides to see Hyde for himself. Waiting by the door, he eventually meets Hyde. He finds him as repellent as Enfield had said he was.

- Utterson goes to Jekyll's house and learns from his servant, Poole, that they all have instructions to obey Hyde, and that he has a key to Jekyll's laboratory.

- Utterson is convinced that Hyde is blackmailing Jekyll. He determines to find out some secret about Hyde's life to help his friend protect himself.

WHY IS THIS CHAPTER IMPORTANT?

A   We learn of Jekyll's strange **will**, which lies at the centre of the mystery of the **relationship** between Jekyll and Hyde.

B   It introduces Lanyon and his **disagreement** with Jekyll over their differing views of **science**. Science is an important theme in the novella.

C   We first encounter **Hyde**, and see that he is as **unnatural** as Enfield said.

D   The idea that Hyde is **blackmailing Jekyll** begins to be treated as a fact.

TOP TIP (A01)

Utterson makes a joke about Hyde's name: 'If he be Mr Hyde … I shall be Mr Seek' (p. 11). Hyde's name might have been chosen because he is a way of 'hiding' the darker aspects of Jekyll's personality. The name 'Jekyll' might be broken into 'je kill', with 'je' being the French for 'I'.

KEY THEME: JEKYLL'S WILL (A02)

As Jekyll's lawyer, Utterson is responsible for looking after his will and making sure it is carried out if Jekyll dies. The will is unusual, and it disturbs Utterson that he does not know Hyde. Once he has met Hyde, it disturbs him that Hyde is unpleasant. His fear that Hyde is blackmailing Jekyll becomes a firm belief, and he turns to an illegal remedy – hoping to find out something that Hyde has done which he could hold over him, countering his supposed threat to Jekyll.

CHECKPOINT 2 (A01)

What do we learn of Lanyon in this chapter?

KEY THEME: SCIENCE (A02)

Lanyon and Jekyll disagree about what constitutes science. Lanyon dismisses Jekyll's interests as 'unscientific balderdash' (p. 10) that had become 'too fanciful' (p. 9) for Lanyon. Although Utterson thinks that the pair have 'only differed on some point of science' (p. 10), it is much more than this. The **novella** questions the very nature of science – is it the entirely practical and understandable pursuit that Lanyon thinks it is, or can it involve the mysteries of the mind and spirit, as Jekyll believes?

KEY CONTEXT (A03)

In Greek legend, Damon and Pathias (or Pythius) are close friends. Pathius is sentenced to death for plotting against the king of Syracuse, Dionysius I. Damon offers to take his place while Pathius returns home to say goodbye to his family. Pathius is late returning, having been attacked by pirates, and Damon is about to die when he arrives. Impressed by their friendship, Dionysius pardons them both.

KEY CONTEXT: DAMON AND PATHIUS (A03)

In the eighteenth and nineteenth centuries, Damon and Pathius were used as an example of faithful friendship, so when Lanyon says the difference between himself and Jekyll 'would have estranged Damon and Pythias' (p. 10) he means that it was much more than a minor argument about a point of science.

AIMING HIGH: INTRODUCING JEKYLL'S DUAL NATURE

Look out for clues in the narrative that hint at themes or ideas taken up later. At this point in the novella we have still not met Jekyll. In Chapter 1, Enfield described him as the 'pink of the proprieties, celebrated too' (p. 5) and here Utterson says he 'was wild when he was young' (p. 15). These two contrasting views prepare us for the dual nature of Jekyll, and his own account of how he felt a division between his respectable, public self and the part of him that enjoyed guilty pleasures.

KEY QUOTATION: THE HORROR OF HYDE (A01)

Despite Enfield's warning, Utterson is unprepared for the 'hitherto unknown disgust, loathing and fear' (p. 13) which he feels on seeing Hyde: 'God bless me, the man seems hardly human! Something troglodytic, shall we say? or can it be the old story of Dr Fell? or is it the mere radiance of a foul soul that thus transpires through, and transfigures, its clay continent?' (p. 14).

He goes on to say that he sees 'Satan's signature' on Hyde's face. The language used is of things unnatural. A troglodyte is a cave-dweller, and the word is often used to mean a cave-man or type of troll. Dr Fell is the subject of a nursery rhyme about a person disliked for no obvious reason. The combination of 'less than human', 'troglodytic', 'foul soul' and 'Dr Fell' reinforces an impression of something inhumanly awful.

KEY CONTEXT: DR FELL (A03)

A nursery rhyme written in 1680 is about Dr John Fell (1625–86), Bishop of Oxford:

> I do not like thee, Dr Fell,
> The reason why – I cannot tell;
> But this I know, and know full well,
> I do not like thee, Doctor Fell.

His name has been used several times for an unaccountably repellent person, and Stevenson is drawing on this tradition.

KEY SETTING: JEKYLL'S HOUSE (A02)

Utterson walks from the shabby door to Jekyll's house, just round the corner. Jekyll's house is in a street of previously grand houses now neglected and run down, but his alone has 'a great air of wealth and comfort' (p. 14). It is a house Utterson enjoys visiting, with a hall he considers 'the pleasantest room in London' (p. 14), comfortably warmed by a fire and with a stone floor. Yet the house is connected to 'the old dissecting room' (p. 15), which lies behind the door Hyde used. The contrast of the welcoming hall with a dissecting room, where a previous doctor used to cut up dead bodies, is unsettling and casts a shadow over the pleasant setting of Jekyll's hall. Jekyll's house has a dual aspect, just as he does.

REVISION FOCUS: JEKYLL'S HOUSE AND LABORATORY

Chapter 1 includes a description of the door Hyde uses and the courtyard it is near (p. 2), and a description of the view from the courtyard on page 6. Chapter 2 includes an account of Utterson walking from the door to Jekyll's house, which is around a corner. The house connects to the laboratory (later Utterson and Poole cross the courtyard from the house to get to it).

Draw a rough sketch of the layout and appearance of the buildings. This will help you to visualise later events in this location.

KEY CONTEXT (A03)

Utterson remarks, 'if ever I read Satan's signature upon a face, it is on that of your new friend' (p. 14). The belief that a person's character or moral standing was evident in the features of their face was common in the nineteenth century. It was expected that evil people or criminals would be ugly. The pseudo-science of physiognomy relied on reading the face to uncover character.

CHAPTER THREE: DR JEKYLL WAS QUITE AT EASE

SUMMARY

- Utterson goes to Jekyll's house for a dinner with friends. He stays behind when others leave, taking the chance to talk to Jekyll about his will.
- Jekyll tries to change the subject to his dislike of Lanyon.
- Utterson tells Jekyll he has talked to Hyde. He offers to help Jekyll escape from whatever trouble has him mixed up with Hyde.
- Jekyll refuses to talk about the matter, saying Utterson does not and cannot understand, but that he can be rid of Hyde if he wants. He repeats his demand that if he disappears Utterson must look after Hyde's interests.
- Utterson has no choice but to agree to Jekyll's requests, but reasserts his dislike for the situation.

WHY IS THIS CHAPTER IMPORTANT?

A We first encounter Jekyll in **person** after hearing **accounts** of him from other characters.

B The **split** between Jekyll and Lanyon is reinforced, this time with Jekyll's view of their **difference of opinion**.

C Jekyll gives various clues as to his **relationship** with Hyde. These do not make much sense to us or to Utterson at this point, but looking back they show that at this point Jekyll still **believed** he was in **control** of the **situation**.

KEY CHARACTER: DR HENRY JEKYLL

Jekyll has been mentioned by Enfield in Chapter 1 and Lanyon in Chapter 2, but now we see him for the first time. While Enfield's account of him was favourable, and Lanyon's unfavourable, the narrator gives an account that combines both elements: 'something of a slyish cast perhaps, but every mark of capacity and kindness' (p. 17). Being sly is not a pleasant characteristic. It suggests there is something underhand or devious about Jekyll. Although everyone has a mix of good and bad aspects to their personality, this immediate acknowledgement of contrasting aspects in Jekyll is significant as the duality of his character is a main theme of the novella. The ground is prepared for developing this theme right from his first introduction.

TOP TIP (A01)

Utterson meets with Jekyll's friends who are 'all judges of good wine' (p. 17). This recalls the narrator's comment about Utterson that he 'drank gin when he was alone, to mortify a taste for vintages' (p. 1). We have already been prepared for him enjoying fine wine in the company of his friends.

KEY QUOTATION: JEKYLL'S OPINION OF LANYON (A01)

In Chapter 2, Lanyon says how he has fallen out with Jekyll. Now we have Jekyll's view of the matter. He is scathing in his criticism of Lanyon: 'a hide-bound pedant … an ignorant, blatant pedant. I was never more disappointed in any man than in Lanyon' (p. 17). A 'pedant' is someone who is very particular about details, and especially the accuracy of facts. Jekyll sees Lanyon's unwillingness to entertain any unconventional ideas as being 'hide-bound' (restricted in his views). The term 'hide-bound' is certain to make us think of Hyde. Jekyll's use of the term perhaps shows that Hyde is always on his mind, even when he is apparently relaxing with friends. It is, in fact, Jekyll who is 'Hyde-bound'.

CHECKPOINT 3 (A01)

What more do we learn about Utterson's character in this chapter?

KEY THEME: JEKYLL'S WILL (A02)

The strange details of Jekyll's will were revealed in Chapter 2. This chapter stresses its role as a source of tension between Jekyll and Utterson. In trying to reassure Utterson, Jekyll twice uses ambiguous phrasing. He says 'if I am taken away' and 'when I am no longer here' (p. 19). These could be **euphemisms** for dying, but as the will specifies 'disappearance or unexplained absence' (p. 8), it is also possible that Jekyll is using it **literally**. Later, the oddness of Jekyll's stress on disappearance will strike Utterson forcefully, but he appears to miss the reference here.

EXAM FOCUS: WRITING ABOUT TENSION AND DRAMA (A02)

You might be asked to write about moments of increased tension or drama in the novella and how Stevenson creates these effects. Read this example of a student's account of how Jekyll responds to Utterson saying he has spoken to Hyde:

A clear statement about point of view

This passage is told from Utterson's point of view. Instead of telling us how Jekyll felt, the narrator describes the change in Jekyll's appearance: he first grows pale, then his eyes darken. This is what Utterson sees so we, like Utterson, have to work out what it reveals about Jekyll's state of mind. This is more dramatic than telling us that Jekyll was horrified, or afraid.

Explains the choice the author has made – to describe an external effect instead of an internal state

Shows how this maintains the point of view

Now you try it:

Complete this passage by adding a line about how Jekyll's response adds to the drama.

CHAPTER FOUR: THE CAREW MURDER CASE

SUMMARY

- The murder of Sir Danvers Carew by Hyde is revealed, told from the point of view of a maid who saw it happen and recognised Hyde. Because she fainted, she was not able to report the murder until long afterwards. Half of a broken walking stick and a letter addressed to Utterson were found by the body.
- Utterson identifies the body of Carew and goes with the police officer, Inspector Newcomen, to Hyde's rooms in a poor part of London.
- Utterson and Newcomen search Hyde's rooms. They find them well stocked with fine wines and pictures, but recently ransacked and with ashes in the fire from burned papers. They find the other part of the broken walking stick and part of a burned cheque book.
- At the bank, Newcomen discovers that Hyde has several thousand pounds. Newcomen is, though, unable to find out anything about Hyde, his family, or anyone who knows him.

WHY IS THIS CHAPTER IMPORTANT?

A The **murder** of Carew is a **turning point** for Jekyll, though we do not learn this until later. For Utterson, the murder confirms his fears about the **terrible character** of Hyde.

B The maid's **identification** of Hyde means that Hyde is now **wanted** for **murder**.

TOP TIP (A01)

The maid watches the meeting between Hyde and Carew from her window, and it appears she is too far away to hear what is said as she infers from gesture that Carew is asking the way. Yet under Hyde's blows, 'the bones were audibly shattered' (p. 21). If she could not hear speech, she certainly could not hear breaking bones. Is she exaggerating her testimony, or is the narrator misrepresenting it to increase the horror of the event?

CHECKPOINT 4 (A01)

How does Utterson know where Hyde lives?

KEY CONTEXT: LONDON FOG (A03)

London experienced terrible, thick, poisonous fogs throughout the second half of the nineteenth and first half of the twentieth centuries, caused by air pollution. Stevenson uses the fog to make the setting particularly sinister. In reality, the fog did provide cover for criminals, including Jack the Ripper (the 'Whitechapel Murderer'), who killed at least five women two years after the publication of *Jekyll and Hyde*. The fog is described as a 'chocolate-coloured pall' (p. 22) and 'as brown as umber' (p. 23). As it comes and goes, there is an eerie sense of what is unseen. When there are breaks in the fog, 'a district of some city in a nightmare' is revealed (p. 22).

KEY SETTING: VICTORIAN LONDON (A03)

Hyde's house is in Soho, a part of London that was associated with crime and immoral living in the Victorian period. Utterson sees 'a dingy street' (p. 22) and 'many ragged children' (p. 23) as well as women going out to drink gin early in the morning. This is characteristic of poor areas of London at the time. Houses were tiny, squalid and overcrowded, so people spent a lot of time out on the streets, even when it was very cold. The area seems ideally suited to Hyde's character – a dark place, full of crime and despair. It is in sharp contrast with Jekyll's pleasant house described in Chapter 3.

> **CHECKPOINT 5** (A01)
>
> What function does the maid serve in the narrative?

TOP TIP: PRESENTING VIOLENCE (A01)

The murder of Carew is an apparently random act of terrifying violence, carried out in the dark in what appears to be a fit of madness. The details of the broken ornate walking stick, the sickening sound of breaking bones, the fainting maid and the unnatural Hyde with his air of indefinable deformity are all characteristic of the Gothic tradition.

AIMING HIGH: UNNERVING INSIGHTS

Look out for small details that cast extra light on an incident or character. Utterson is a well-balanced and dependable character, yet the narrator tells us that on the drive through the fog 'he was conscious of some touch of that terror of the law and the law's officers, which may at times assail the most honest' (p. 22). This insight is particularly arresting because we don't expect fanciful thought or unfounded anxiety of Utterson. As he is a lawyer, we would not expect him to feel 'terror of the law'. This shows that he is genuinely unnerved by his journey and what he sees.

In addition, acknowledging a feeling which most people have but rarely talk about involves a degree of intimacy and revelation that the narrator does not usually show. It makes Utterson's unease more striking, and the setting even more unsettling.

> **KEY CONTEXT** (A03)
>
> As Utterson travels to Hyde's house he sees evidence of the poverty of people living in the area. The shops sell 'penny numbers and twopenny salads' (p. 23) – cheap, shocking stories (penny numbers) and meagre salads made largely of root vegetables.

CHAPTER FIVE: INCIDENT OF THE LETTER

SUMMARY

- Utterson goes to visit Jekyll and finds him pale with shock and illness, sitting in his 'cabinet' (p. 25) – a room above his laboratory.
- Jekyll says he has heard people outside shouting about the murder of Carew, implying that this is how he knows about it.
- Jekyll assures Utterson he will have no more to do with Hyde, and is confident that Hyde will disappear.
- Jekyll shows Utterson a letter signed 'Edward Hyde' that he says was hand delivered. It thanks Jekyll for his past generosity and says he can escape safely. Utterson is relieved and regrets assuming Hyde was blackmailing Jekyll.
- Utterson takes the letter home and shows it to his head clerk, Mr Guest. Guest is an expert in analysing handwriting. A servant comes in with a note from Jekyll. Comparing the two documents, Guest notices that the handwriting is similar.
- Utterson leaps to a new conclusion – that Jekyll forged the letter from Hyde, writing it himself.

WHY IS THIS CHAPTER IMPORTANT?

A Utterson first visits Jekyll's **cabinet** and **laboratory**, introducing this important setting.

B The effect of the **murder** on Jekyll is revealed, as he assures Utterson he will have nothing more to do with Hyde.

C Guest's skill at interpreting **handwriting** uncovers the first clue that there is a more complex and mysterious **link** between Jekyll and Hyde.

KEY SETTING: JEKYLL'S LABORATORY AND CABINET (A02)

Utterson reaches Jekyll's laboratory by going through the courtyard mentioned in Chapter 1. The laboratory was used by the previous owner to carry out dissections of dead bodies to teach his anatomy students. This sinister history adds to the Gothic atmosphere (see below). The theatre still has a dismal air; it is 'gaunt and silent' (p. 25), littered with packing cases and straw, and with Jekyll's chemical apparatus all around. The cabinet is behind a door covered with red baize – a type of fuzzy fabric attached to doors to deaden noise. The room contrasts with Jekyll's pleasant hall. It is darkened by fog, has dusty, barred windows, and is cold (Jekyll huddles close to the fire). The iron bars, noise-reducing baize and the cheval glass (a tilting, full-length mirror) gain relevance later when we learn what happens in this room.

KEY STRUCTURE: HYDE'S LETTER (A02)

The letter signed by Hyde is the second significant document in the novella. Documents are used to communicate vital information, and are an important element in the structure of the story. In this case, the letter reveals the similarity between the handwriting of Jekyll and Hyde. Utterson reaches the wrong conclusion, assuming that Jekyll forged the letter for Hyde. This is one of many errors that help to keep the mystery going.

KEY STYLE: GOTHIC (A01)

The unsettling previous history of the dissecting room, the fog that creeps indoors, the barred windows and Jekyll 'looking deadly sick' (p. 25) all contribute to the Gothic atmosphere of the scene. In addition, this chapter uses rich, picturesque and extravagant language which is typical of Gothic literature: 'The fog still slept on the wing above the drowned city, where the lamps glimmered like carbuncles' (p. 28). A carbuncle is a glowing coal, or a fiery-coloured precious stone – but it is also a large boil or abscess that leaks pus. This description combines the appealing imagery of a

warm, glowing light and the idea of sleeping on the wing (like a migrating bird) with the repellent 'drowned' city studded with boils. This is another example of the duality associated with Jekyll.

REVISION FOCUS: JEKYLL'S SECRET

This chapter contains some subtle clues as to the nature of the relationship between Jekyll and Hyde, the most significant of which is the similarity between their handwriting. Look carefully at the wording of Jekyll's speech and pick out ways in which he avoids lying but still misleads Utterson.

Find evidence in earlier chapters of the true nature of the link between Jekyll and Hyde.

CHECKPOINT 6 (A01)

How does Utterson get to Jekyll's cabinet? The details of the route are important as he uses the same route later in the story.

TOP TIP (A01)

The sentence starting 'In the bottle, the acids were long ago resolved' (p. 28) is an ornate and complex description of the fine wine that Utterson has been drinking with Guest, in keeping with his 'taste for vintages' (p. 1). The long, poetic description is indulgent and slow, creating a sense of the mellow, relaxed evening.

CHAPTER SIX: REMARKABLE INCIDENT OF DR LANYON

SUMMARY

- Although a large reward has been offered for Hyde, he has disappeared. For two months, Jekyll returns to his old self, being sociable and renewing his friendship with Lanyon.

- Jekyll suddenly refuses to see Utterson again, alarming the lawyer. Utterson visits Lanyon and finds him physically changed and clearly disturbed by something terrifying.

- Lanyon refuses to talk about Jekyll, saying that he regards him as dead. Utterson is puzzled, and writes to Jekyll asking why he will not see either Utterson or Lanyon. Jekyll's reply is mysterious, but reinforces Lanyon's statement that the two will never see each other again.

- Less than two weeks later, Lanyon dies. Utterson receives a package addressed to him by Lanyon. It contains a letter and an envelope, which the letter says is not to be opened until Jekyll dies or disappears. This reference to disappearance again makes Utterson curious, but he puts the package in his safe.

- Utterson tries to see Jekyll several times, but is increasingly relieved when he is turned away. Poole tells him that Jekyll spends more and more time in his cabinet and laboratory, and seems preoccupied and unhappy.

WHY IS THIS CHAPTER IMPORTANT?

A Hyde seems to have **disappeared** without trace, and Jekyll's mood lightens, reinforcing the suggestion that the link between them is **damaging** to Jekyll.

B Lanyon dies, first suffering a severe physical and emotional **change**. We know only that this has something to do with Jekyll, so it heightens the **mystery** surrounding him.

C Utterson receives another strange **letter** referring to the **disappearance** of Jekyll.

D Jekyll becomes increasingly **reclusive** and **troubled**.

KEY QUOTATION: HYDE'S DISAPPEARANCE

After Hyde's disappearance, the narrator says that more was discovered about Hyde's terrible past:

'Much of his past was unearthed, indeed, and all disreputable: tales came out of the man's cruelty, at once so callous and violent, of his vile life, of his strange associates, of the hatred that seemed to have surrounded his career' (p. 30).

This account seems, with hindsight, to be unreliable. 'Much of his past' suggests he has had as much past as anyone else, yet Hyde does not exist most of the time; he has not had a career; he has few or no associates; and he has only existed since Jekyll started to take the potion. The use of the word 'tales' hints that the accounts might be fanciful – either made up or exaggerated. When Newcomen investigated Hyde, nothing could be discovered about him. It appears that the narrator has been taken in by false reports and conjecture. If so, this is the only example of the narrator being unreliable in his own voice rather than reporting wrong assumptions made by other characters. It helps to maintain the mystery and our false beliefs about Hyde, but it might be considered dishonest or cheating for Stevenson to use the otherwise reliable narrator in this way.

CHECKPOINT 7 **A01**

How do Lanyon's appearance and manner in this chapter compare with how he has been presented before?

TOP TIP **A02**

Notice how the rapidity of the decline in Lanyon and Jekyll is stressed by the precise dates given. The precision of this detail is another distraction from the mystery of what is going on. You could draw up a mini timeline to keep track of how these two characters decline.

KEY THEME: CONJECTURE

Utterson finds Lanyon physically depleted and with 'a look in the eye and quality of manner that seemed to testify to some deep-seated terror of the mind' (p. 31). He leaps to the conclusion that Lanyon, as a doctor, has recognised signs of a serious illness in himself and is afraid of dying. This is another in the series of wrong assumptions that Utterson makes that distracts our attention from what is really happening.

KEY THEME: MYSTERY **A02**

The mysteries of Jekyll's relapse into solitude and of Lanyon's sudden illness are followed by the letter Lanyon leaves for Utterson and the reminder of Jekyll's strange will. Although events are documented with precision, what they mean is left to conjecture. In the case of the letter, no explanation is offered and the chapter ends with a sense of unsettling mystery.

Lanyon's view of life seems to have changed, with his previous certainty and confidence in science shaken. His statement 'if we knew all, we should be more glad to get away' (p. 31) means that there are mysteries we generally know nothing about, and that they are so terrible they make death seem attractive. This is a view he would have dismissed before. It is repeated by Jekyll, who says 'I could not think that this earth contained a place for sufferings and terrors so unmanning' (p. 32). These two references to unspecified horrors increase the sense of mystery in the novella, raise the tension, and contribute to its Gothic atmosphere.

CHAPTER SEVEN: INCIDENT AT THE WINDOW

SUMMARY

- On another of his Sunday walks with Enfield, Utterson tells his companion that he once saw Hyde and felt the same sense of revulsion as Enfield had described.
- Enfield reveals that he has since found out that the door is the rear entry to Jekyll's laboratory.
- The pair come to the courtyard near the door to Jekyll's laboratory and step into it. They see Jekyll sitting at an upstairs window and call up to him.
- They encourage him to come and walk with them, but Jekyll refuses. He says his room is not fit for them to visit, so they cannot come up either. They then say they will stand and talk with him. Jekyll at first agrees, but a look of horror soon crosses his face and he draws back from the window.
- Appalled at what they have seen in Jekyll's face, Enfield and Utterson walk away.

CHECKPOINT 8 (A02)

Why does Utterson say 'God forgive us, God forgive us' (p. 35)?

WHY IS THIS CHAPTER IMPORTANT?

A The **horror** that Jekyll experiences is made evident here in the response of Enfield and Utterson, too **shocked** by the change they have seen in his face even to speak until they have gone some distance away.

B This is the **last time** that Utterson will see Jekyll.

AIMING HIGH: THE OBJECTIVE CORRELATIVE

Look out for more advanced types of literary device. Writers often use settings, weather, objects or other external features to reflect the feelings of characters. In this chapter, the courtyard to Jekyll's house is described as 'very cool and a little damp, and full of premature twilight' (p. 34) even though the sky above is bright. By making Jekyll's personal space dark and dank, Stevenson represents Jekyll's internal state in his external setting. This technique is called the objective correlative.

Throughout the book, Stevenson uses fog, damp, gloomy light, darkness and cold to help convey sombre moods. They contribute to the Gothic atmosphere of the book but also relate directly to the frame of mind of the characters and the darkness of the deeds described.

KEY STRUCTURE: THE MID-POINT

This chapter recalls the very beginning of the novella, with Enfield and Utterson walking together and coming to the same door. The first incident began the narrative of Hyde and this one, Utterson hopes, marks its end. It is the halfway point of the novella, and would be a suitable place to mark an ending – but the chapter finishes with an unsettling incident that makes it quite clear that the story is far from finished.

KEY LANGUAGE: THE LANGUAGE OF HORROR

The previous chapter has intensified the sense of mystery, and this chapter renews and increases the feeling of horror. This raises the tension before the account of the events of the final night. Jekyll's face takes on an expression of 'such abject terror and despair' (p. 35) that it freezes the blood of Enfield and Utterson. This is typically extravagant Gothic language; 'terror' and 'despair' are both words that feature a lot in Gothic literature as well as being major themes of it. The impact on Utterson and Enfield is shown in their response – to walk away silently before Utterson calls on God's forgiveness.

Stevenson stresses the horror Utterson and Enfield feel by having them walk away before speaking – they want to put some distance between themselves and the scene, to re-enter the reassuring bustle of normal life. Physically turning away from what they have seen echoes their desire for emotional distance.

REVISION FOCUS: ENFIELD

This is the second and last time that Enfield appears in the novella. Look back at his first appearance, and compare it with this one. What can you say about his character in Chapter 1? Is it consistent with how he behaves and speaks in this chapter? Are there any ways in which he has changed?

KEY LANGUAGE: JEKYLL AS PRISONER

> **KEY CONTEXT** A03
>
> Jekyll sits at a half-open window, which he then 'thrust down' (p. 35). A window that is closed downwards is a sash window, common in Victorian houses. The window slides up and down in its frame, not opening either into the room or out into the street. This is necessary, as the windows are crossed by iron bars.

Jekyll is described as sitting by the open window, 'with an infinite sadness of mien, like some disconsolate prisoner' (p. 34). 'Mien' means facial appearance, indicating mood. He is described as being *like* a prisoner, which is a simile. Although this is presented as a simile, it seems that Jekyll actually *is* a prisoner. He is unable to leave his room – he says 'it is quite impossible; I dare not' (p. 35) – and the windows are barred, as we know from Utterson's visit to the cabinet: 'three dusty windows barred with iron' (p. 25).

CHAPTER EIGHT: THE LAST NIGHT

SUMMARY

- Poole visits Utterson, asking him to come with him as he fears something is wrong with Jekyll. The two go to Jekyll's laboratory and knock, but a voice from inside refuses to let Utterson in.

- Poole says that he fears Jekyll was murdered eight days before, when he heard him cry out, and that the murderer is still in the cabinet. He has seen the man once and he was very short and wearing a mask. He believes it was Hyde.

- Utterson and Poole arm themselves with a poker and an axe and go to break down the door. The footman, Bradshaw, goes to cover the back door in case Hyde tries to escape. Utterson and Poole hear someone pacing in the cabinet.

- Utterson announces their intention to break into the room and Hyde's voice calls out, begging them not to. Utterson and Poole break down the door.

- They find the body of Hyde, dressed in clothes too big for him, still twitching on the floor. They hunt the premises but cannot find Jekyll's corpse.

- They find an envelope addressed to Utterson. It contains: a new will, in Utterson's favour; a note telling Utterson to read the letter he has from Lanyon; and a long letter from Jekyll. They lock up the cabinet with Hyde's body inside and Utterson goes home to read the documents.

CHECKPOINT 9 **A02**

How does Utterson behave towards Poole?

WHY IS THIS CHAPTER IMPORTANT?

A This is the climax of the novella, with Hyde's death.

B The mystery deepens, but looks at last to be resolved with the document that Utterson takes away to read.

KEY CONTEXT: POISON

Utterson realises that Hyde is a 'self-destroyer' (p. 45), meaning he has killed himself. The strong smell of 'kernels' alerts him to this. Kernels are the central seeds inside fruits and nuts. They are a source of cyanide, a type of poisonous chemical that can cause death in seconds. The rapid death makes it convenient for Hyde as he can take it as soon as he realises he is doomed. Jekyll's work with chemicals makes it plausible that cyanide is available to Hyde.

TOP TIP (A01)

Look back at Chapter 5 when Utterson first goes to Jekyll's cabinet. He follows the same route with Poole, so Stevenson does not need to spell it out this time.

KEY QUOTATION: A WILD NIGHT (A01)

As Utterson and Poole walk to Jekyll's house, it is a 'wild, cold, seasonable night of March, with a pale moon, lying on her back as though the wind had tilted her, and a flying wrack of the most diaphanous and lawny texture' (p. 37). This poetic description does not at first seem in keeping with the urgency of their mission. But it creates a feeling of unearthliness, with strange powers at work. For the moon to have been apparently blown over by the wind, for the night to be 'wild', suggests this will be an extraordinary night. The 'flying wrack' means clouds moving quickly. The description 'diaphanous and lawny' means they were thin and filmy. The fast-moving tatters of clouds are carried by the wind, adding to the sense of stronger-than-human powers at work in an eerie atmosphere.

CHECKPOINT 10 (A01)

There is a cheval glass in Jekyll's cabinet. This is a mirror that pivots in a frame so that it can swing vertically. When Utterson and Poole find it, the mirror is tilted towards the ceiling so that the reflection of someone in the room would not be seen. Why is this?

KEY CHARACTER: UTTERSON (A02)

In this chapter, we see the most extended interaction of Utterson with another character, Poole. Utterson's character is reinforced and developed through this. He is 'inclined to be irritated' (p. 36) when he is frightened by Poole saying he fears foul play. A practical and active man, he takes up his hat and coat immediately when Poole asks him to go to Jekyll's house. Utterson expects conventional behaviour from Jekyll's servants and considers it 'Very irregular, very unseemly' (p. 38) that they are gathered together.

In keeping with his profession as a lawyer, Utterson always looks for a rational, straightforward explanation of any situation. He dismisses Poole's suggestion that the murderer is still in Jekyll's cabinet, because 'That won't hold water; it doesn't commend itself to reason' (p. 39). His interpretation of Jekyll frantically trying to get hold of a supply of a chemical, wearing a mask and acting desperately, is that he has a disfiguring disease he is trying to treat (p. 41). Utterson is inclined to treat his guesses and assumptions as established facts, though, and acts as though they were certainties. Finally, he is a man of action, responds practically under pressure and in unusual circumstances and is not flustered, even by finding Hyde's body.

KEY CONTEXT: SOCIAL CLASS **A03**

Utterson speaks to Jekyll's servants as he might speak to his own. He criticises their behaviour in clustering in the hall, and he speaks sharply to Poole, asking him why Jekyll's note to the pharmacist is not sealed.

Utterson addresses Poole by his surname, and he takes charge of the situation, telling the servants what to do as they plan their assault on Jekyll's cabinet. They obey him without question and without doubting his authority and right to tell them what to do.

All this is in keeping with the way someone of Utterson's social standing would behave towards servants, considered his social inferiors. His behaviour and language towards the servants helps to establish him as a figure of similar social standing to Jekyll and Lanyon.

TOP TIP **A01**

Compare the scene in Jekyll's cabinet this time with Utterson's previous visit. Draw up a table with two columns to record similarities and differences.

EXAM FOCUS: WRITING ABOUT EFFECTS **A02**

You might be asked to distinguish between episodes that are narrated directly, or are recorded in documents or described afterwards by characters, and what effect this creates. Read this student response to a question about action scenes.

> *Relates the scene under discussion to the rest of the novella*

> *Illustration of point with quotation*

There are relatively few moments of action in the novella which are described directly rather than recalled by a character or described in a document. One of these is when Utterson and Poole break into Jekyll's cabinet. Stevenson uses verbs that create a sense of vigorous activity: the blow 'shook' the building, the door 'leaped', the axe 'crashed' and the lock finally 'burst in sunder'. 'Leaped' is a verb we associate with humans, not objects. By using it of an object, Stevenson makes the scene more lively, as though the energy comes from the things.

> *Explains effects of choice of words*

> *Good attempt to extend discussion of effect*

Now you try it:

Add to this answer by saying something about other effects created with language in this passage, such as rhythm or repetition.

KEY STRUCTURE: JEKYLL'S DOCUMENTS **A01**

Documents are an important part of the way the action is narrated. There are four documents mentioned in this chapter: the replacement will, which names Utterson in place of Hyde to inherit from Jekyll; the note from Jekyll; Lanyon's letter; and Jekyll's statement. These last two documents will form the final chapters of the book. As Utterson goes to read them, the main narrative ends.

CHAPTER NINE: DR LANYON'S NARRATIVE

SUMMARY

- The whole chapter is in the form of a letter from Lanyon, including within it a letter from Jekyll to Lanyon. Jekyll's letter asks Lanyon to leave everything he is doing and go to Jekyll's house where Poole will be waiting with a locksmith to break into the cabinet. Lanyon is to find a particular drawer, take it back to his own house and wait for a visitor at midnight.

- The letter makes clear that Jekyll's life and sanity rely on Lanyon doing as he has asked him. Lanyon suspects it is evidence of Jekyll's madness, but carries out the instructions. The drawer contains a collection of chemicals and a book recording dates and brief notes.

- At midnight, Hyde comes to Lanyon's house. Lanyon is instantly repelled by him, especially when Hyde touches his arm.

- Hyde is impatient for the drawer, which Lanyon soon gives to him, and mixes a potion using chemicals from it.

- Hyde gives Lanyon the choice of letting him walk outside with the potion in the glass or watch as he takes it. Lanyon chooses to watch.

- Lanyon is horrified to see the effect on Hyde, but more horrified still as he watches Hyde transform into Jekyll.

TOP TIP (A01)

Lanyon states that he received Jekyll's letter on 9 January, but the letter as presented is dated 10 December. This is probably an error on Stevenson's part – he has been inconsistent when working on the last version of the text.

WHY IS THIS CHAPTER IMPORTANT?

A This chapter holds the key to the novella – it reveals that Jekyll and Hyde are the **same person**, or two aspects of the same person, and that a chemical **potion** is the means of switching between the two.

B It is the first extended first-person narrative in the book.

C It reveals more about the **character** of Lanyon and about the nature of his **disagreement** with Jekyll about **science**.

CHECKPOINT 11 (A02)

Lanyon asks of Jekyll, 'If his messenger could go to one place, why could he not go to another?' (p. 52). Why does Hyde not go directly to Jekyll's cabinet himself?

TOP TIP (A01)

On page 52, Lanyon presents a series of questions that he asked himself when he read Jekyll's letter. A question that someone asks without expecting an answer is called a rhetorical question. Stevenson uses this device to direct our thinking about the story and to increase the sense of mystery as we ponder the same questions.

KEY THEME: SCIENCE (A01)

Science is the most important theme in this chapter. The events are narrated by Lanyon, who is a medical doctor and is interested in conventional, rational science. He is the best person to tell this part of the story as he has most understanding of the activity.

He tries to give a clinical account of what is odd about Hyde: a 'remarkable combination of great muscular activity and great apparent debility of constitution' (p. 53). He also tries to describe the physical effect that Hyde has on him: an 'incipient rigor' (stiffening) and 'a marked sinking of the pulse' (p. 53). But this is not adequate. It describes the physical symptoms but does not account for the revulsion everyone feels on seeing Hyde.

Lanyon gives a clinical account of the changes that come over Hyde after he drinks the potion, too, but the horror of the transformation soon overwhelms him.

EXAM FOCUS: WRITING ABOUT SCIENCE (A01)

Key point	Evidence/Further meaning
● Stevenson does not name the chemicals Jekyll uses, but makes them sound convincing by using scientific language and referring to some chemical components.	● The potion is made from a 'blood-red liquor' (p. 52), called a 'tincture' (p. 55), and a 'crystalline salt of a white colour' (p. 51). ● To Lanyon's practised senses the liquid seemed to contain 'phosphorus and some volatile ether' (p. 52).
● When combined, the liquid and crystals fizz, produce fumes and change colour – all dramatic but realistic effects of chemical reactions.	● The account uses scientific terminology, and is given in moderate, measured language like the language of a science textbook. ● The mixture starts to 'effervesce' (fizz), and when the 'ebullition' (bubbling) stops, it changes colour (p. 55). ● The 'metamorphoses' (changes) stop when it is a 'watery green' (p. 55).
● Hyde uses a graduated glass to measure 'a few minims' (p. 55) – he is apparently following proper scientific procedure.	● A graduated glass is marked with a scale for measuring liquids. However, a minim is only around 1/100 of a teaspoon, so there would not be enough to watch fizzing and changing colour. ● Stevenson clearly intended there to be more potion, as Hyde drinks it 'at one gulp' (p. 55).

AIMING HIGH: LINKS WITH THE LEGEND OF FAUST

Look for connections with other texts or stories. The danger of forbidden knowledge is an ancient theme. In the Old Testament, Adam and Eve are exiled from Paradise after eating the fruit of the Tree of Knowledge. It is also the theme of the legend of Faust, retold by writers including Christopher Marlowe (1564–93) in English and Johann Wolfgang von Goethe (1749–1832) in German. Faust makes a pact with the Devil, trading his soul for twenty years of unlimited knowledge and pleasure. There is a clear link between Jekyll and Faust: Jekyll seeks knowledge beyond regular science and uses it to free part of himself to indulge in whatever pleasures he wishes. Knowledge comes with a high price in *Jekyll and Hyde*. Jekyll loses his reason and his life to his experiment. Hyde asks Lanyon if the 'greed of curiosity' (p. 55) is too great for him to resist, and it is – Lanyon dies, unable to bear what he has learned.

KEY CHARACTER: HYDE A01

Like other characters who encounter him, Lanyon instinctively feels there is something wrong with Hyde, something repellent: 'there was something abnormal and misbegotten in the very essence of the creature' (p. 53). As Lanyon is a medical doctor, we might expect him to be more tolerant than other people of someone with a deformity or illness. His revulsion, like that of the 'Sawbones' in Chapter 1 (p. 4), is an indication that it is not just a physical aspect of Hyde that is repellent. By calling him a 'creature', Lanyon suggests that Hyde is somehow inhuman.

TOP TIP A01

A 'creature' is something that has been created. Hyde has been created from and by Jekyll, by releasing the evil that is part of him to have independent existence.

KEY QUOTATION: THE REALISATION A01

Lanyon's letter reveals that Jekyll and Hyde are the same person. He saves the crucial information for the end of his account:

> 'O God!' I screamed, and 'O God!' again and again; for there before my eyes – pale and shaken, and half fainting, and groping before him with his hands, like a man restored from death – there stood Henry Jekyll! (p. 56)

The revelation is held back until the end of the sentence, the word order managed so that Jekyll's name is the very last thing we read. With the interjection 'O God!', the sentence first communicates Lanyon's horror, then, with 'before my eyes', goes on to what he has seen. But it is impossible for us to visualise it, to see it before our own eyes, because we don't know what the pale, shaken, half-fainting thing is, and even when we know it is a man, we don't yet know who. In this way, the text recreates in us the confusion, suspense and shock that Lanyon experiences.

CHAPTER TEN: HENRY JEKYLL'S FULL STATEMENT OF THE CASE

SUMMARY

- Jekyll gives an account of his history. He was so keen to be well regarded that he hid his pleasures, acting like two different people.
- Jekyll had begun to think about how a person is made up of good and evil parts, then made a potion that could separate the two. As soon as he changed into Hyde he was aware of the evil inside him, but it thrilled him. Taking the potion again, he turned back to Jekyll.
- Jekyll began to take the potion regularly, but Hyde knew no limits. One day he woke as Hyde when he had not taken the potion. Afraid that he would lose the power to turn back, he decided to stop using it.
- After two months, the temptation was too strong and he took it again, and Hyde killed Carew. When Jekyll was himself again, he realised he could no longer dare to use the potion.
- After one day changing into Hyde unexpectedly, Jekyll had to arrange for Lanyon to collect his chemicals so he could change back. As he changed increasingly easily into Hyde, he had to stay in his cabinet and laboratory.
- At last, he ran out of the salt he needed to make his potion, and realised he would become Hyde forever. He wrote his last statement after taking the final dose, uncertain whether Hyde would be caught and hanged or would kill himself before that happened.

CHECKPOINT 12 **A01**

What does Jekyll mean when he says he was committed to 'a profound duplicity of life' (p. 57)?

WHY IS THIS CHAPTER IMPORTANT?

A This is the only time we have Jekyll's **account** of events and a proper **insight** into his character.

B Jekyll's account clears up all the remaining mysteries of the novella, explaining how he came to take the **potion** and free part of his **personality** as Hyde. It reveals the full truth about earlier incidents.

C Two of the most important themes of the novella are fully explored only in this chapter: **duality** and the **good/evil nature** of humankind.

KEY CONTEXT: CAPITAL PUNISHMENT A03

The punishment for murder in the nineteenth century was execution by hanging. When Jekyll says Hyde was 'thrall to the gallows' (p. 70) he means that he would be taken to the gallows (the scaffold from which criminals were hanged) if discovered.

REVISION FOCUS: JEKYLL

Jekyll gives an account of his character on pages 57–8. Draw up a table with a list of points from this account in the first column. Add further columns to add more detail or evidence from what other characters have said about him and his behaviour.

KEY CONTEXT: CAPTIVES OF PHILIPPI A03

After two battles at the Macedonian city of Philippi in AD42, the victorious Roman leaders Antony and Octavian freed captives who had been supporters of the losing side, led by the traitors Cassius and Brutus who had conspired to kill Julius Caesar. Their supporters could have expected death. Stevenson chooses this reference because it suggests Jekyll is freeing someone (or something) that has betrayed him and could do him harm in the future.

KEY QUOTATION: THE DUALITY OF HUMAN NATURE A01

While explaining how he behaved, Jekyll says his aspirations to be taken seriously and respected 'with even a deeper trench than in the majority of men, severed in me those provinces of good and ill which divide and compound man's dual nature' (p. 57).

By this he means that because of how he wanted other people to view him, he divided his nature more than he says most people do. A 'province' is an area of land under a particular jurisdiction, like a county or country. Jekyll uses the word to continue the geographical metaphor that begins with a 'deeper trench'. The image is visual – instead of the abstract aspects of good and evil within a person's mind or soul, we are asked to imagine a landscape split by a vast trench.

That good and ill 'divide and compound' man's nature means that they both split it but also make it complete: Stevenson suggests that we are a compound – an integrated mix – of both good and bad, neither wholly one nor the other. What Jekyll has done in dividing them totally is therefore unnatural.

TOP TIP A01

Jekyll says that when he realised he could not dare to turn into Hyde, who was wanted for murder, he 'ground the key under [his] heel' (p. 68) so that he could no longer use the door from the laboratory to the street. This is the key that Utterson and Poole find crushed and spotted with rust in Chapter 9.

REVISION FOCUS: DOCUMENTS

Documents play an important role in *Jekyll and Hyde*. Draw up a table listing all the documents that feature in the novella, with columns to show who wrote each, what it contains and what its role is in the story.

KEY THEME: GOOD AND EVIL **A01**

Jekyll stresses that the evil which is Hyde is a part of him – that he has simply separated that part from himself and given it freedom. But although 'Hyde, alone in the ranks of mankind, was pure evil' (p. 61), Jekyll keeps the mixed nature that he had before. This suggests that while evil can be given free rein if not kept in check by conscience and discipline, no person can ever be wholly good. Perhaps the reason is that goodness is demonstrated and accomplished by shunning evil, so goodness without evil is impossible.

Dr Henry Jekyll   Mr Edward Hyde

AIMING HIGH: MILTON ON GOOD AND EVIL ⭐

It's important to make connections with other works that Stevenson knew and drew on. The English poet John Milton wrote a long narrative poem called *Paradise Lost*, which deals with the nature of good and evil. He also wrote an essay, titled 'Areopagitica', in which he summarised the way the two are linked:

> Good and evil we know in the field of this world grow up together almost inseparably … It was from out the rind of one apple tasted that the knowledge of good and evil, as two twins cleaving together, leaped forth into the world. And perhaps this is that doom which Adam fell into of knowing good and evil, that is to say of knowing good by evil.
>
> John Milton, 'Areopagitica', 1644

Stevenson knew both works.

TOP TIP **A02**

Jekyll refers to the 'seemingly so solid body' (p. 59). The alliteration of *seemingly so solid* draws attention to the phrase, and recalls a line Hamlet uses in Shakespeare's play, referring to his body as this 'too too solid flesh' (*Hamlet*, Act I, Scene 2). Hamlet wishes his flesh could melt and dissolve – Jekyll finds a way to make it happen.

KEY CONTEXT **A03**

Jekyll describes his first involuntary change into Hyde as being 'like the Babylonian finger on the wall' (p. 65). He is referring to an episode in the Bible in which the king Belshazzar is feasting when a hand appears and writes a warning on the wall foretelling the imminent downfall of the Babylonian empire. Jeykll means the episode warned him that his carefully managed double life was about to end.

KEY CONTEXT: ADDICTION (A03)

The account of how Jekyll becomes increasingly resistant to the effects of his potion, how he has to take larger doses to return himself to normality (to Jekyll) and how he becomes entirely preoccupied with his transitions and his potion is reminiscent of drug addiction. Jekyll becomes 'a creature eaten up and emptied by fever, languidly weak both in body and mind, and solely occupied by one thought' (p. 72). These are feelings that may have been known to Stevenson himself; it has been claimed that he used drugs such as cocaine, and even that he was under its influence when he wrote *The Strange Case of Dr Jekyll and Mr Hyde* rapidly, over six days.

EXAM FOCUS: WRITING ABOUT JEKYLL'S STRUGGLE (A01)

You might be asked to write about Jekyll's account of his dual nature. Read this example of a student's account of how Jekyll uses imagery to explain the two aspects within him:

> Jekyll uses imagery to try to explain how he experiences the sense of being divided within himself. He speaks of Hyde as an animal or 'brute' who is 'caged' or 'chained' in Jekyll and 'comes out roaring' or growling when Jekyll takes his potion. This is a suitable image, as a dangerous caged animal is controllable while contained, but deadly if it escapes; this is exactly what happens in Jekyll's case. Further, after one of Hyde's excursions, he describes two responses within himself – the worse part is satisfied, like an animal licking its chops, while the better part is drowsy ('a little drowsed.').

Identifies words that are used in imagery

Good account of why the imagery is appropriate

Clearly signals to the examiner that it is important to know why an image is used

The adverb 'further' indicates that the point is going to be continued with another example

Now you try it:

Jekyll also uses imagery or clothing to convey how he can go in disguise in Hyde's identity. Add a sentence or two about this imagery and how it works.

PROGRESS AND REVISION CHECK

SECTION ONE: CHECK YOUR KNOWLEDGE

Answer these quick questions to test your basic knowledge of the novella, its characters and events:

1. Where do Utterson and Enfield stop on their Sunday walk, and why?

2. How has Utterson acquired his friends?

3. How much money do the crowd, Utterson and the 'Sawbones' persuade Hyde to give to the family of the injured girl?

4. What is strange about Jekyll's will?

5. Why does Utterson want to find out about Hyde's past?

6. Who is a witness to the murder of Carew?

7. Which item of evidence do Utterson and Newcomen find in Hyde's flat that links him to the murder?

8. What is Guest's special skill that helps Utterson in his investigation of the link between Jekyll and Hyde?

9. What does Lanyon say has caused the change in his health when Utterson visits him to ask about Jekyll?

10. Why does Jekyll suddenly close the window when he is talking to Utterson from it?

11. What is the reason Poole gives for asking Utterson to go with him to Jekyll's house?

12. Which tools do Utterson and Poole take to break down the door to Jekyll's cabinet?

13. Why is Poole certain that it was not Jekyll, but Hyde, that he saw scuttling around the laboratory?

14. What do Poole and Utterson find on the ground near the inside of the door that opens from the street into the laboratory?

15. How does Utterson know that Hyde has killed himself?

16. What is in the drawer which Hyde's letter asks Lanyon to collect from the cabinet and hand over to Hyde?

17. Why does Lanyon decide to watch while Hyde takes the potion?

18. Why does Jekyll set out to make the potion that will produce the transformations?

19. Which event leads Jekyll to decide never to take the potion again, and why?

20. Why is Jekyll unable to make more of his potion?

SECTION TWO: CHECK YOUR UNDERSTANDING

Here are two tasks about the significance of particular moments in the novella. These require more thought and slightly longer responses. In each case, try to write at least three to four paragraphs.

Task 1: Why is the section in Chapter 1 in which Enfield describes his encounter with Hyde important? (Read from '"Well, it was this way," returned Mr Enfield' (p. 3) to 'fell into a vein of musing' (p. 5).) Think about:

- what impression of Hyde we gain from this section
- how it sets up questions that will prompt Utterson's actions.

Task 2: What is the importance of the section in Chapter 8 in which Utterson and Poole break down the door to the cabinet? (Read from 'Poole swung the axe' (p. 44) to 'the dead malefactor stretched upon the carpet' (p. 47).) Think about:

- how the cabinet is portrayed as normal and abnormal in this section
- how the state of the cabinet relates to the state of Jekyll himself.

PROGRESS CHECK

GOOD PROGRESS

I can:

- understand how Stevenson has sequenced and revealed events. ☐
- refer to the importance of key events in the novella. ☐
- select well-chosen evidence, including key quotations, to support my ideas. ☐

EXCELLENT PROGRESS

I can:

- refer in depth to main and minor events and how they contribute to the development of the plot. ☐
- understand how Stevenson has carefully ordered or revealed events for particular effects. ☐
- draw on a range of carefully selected key evidence, including quotations, to support my ideas. ☐

WHO'S WHO?

Dr Hastie Lanyon
Doctor

Mr Richard Enfield
*Mr Utterson's friend
and distant cousin*

Mr Gabriel Utterson
Lawyer

Mr Guest
Mr Utterson's chief clerk

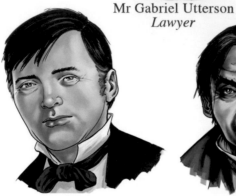

Dr Henry Jekyll

Mr Edward Hyde

Mr Poole
Dr Jekyll's butler

Mr Hyde's Landlady

Sir Danvers Carew
MP murdered by Hyde

Inspector Newcomen

Bradshaw
Dr Jekyll's footman

Maid
witnesses a crime

DR HENRY JEKYLL

JEKYLL'S ROLE IN THE NOVELLA

Dr Henry Jekyll is a medical doctor with an interest in the supernatural. He carries out experiments, and makes a potion that transforms him into his **alter ego**, Hyde. In the **novella** he:

- makes a potion which separates the good and bad aspects of himself and allows him to switch between two identities – those of Jekyll and Hyde. As Hyde, he indulges in secret pleasures, but as Jekyll he lives respectably.
- makes a will leaving everything to Hyde if he dies or disappears.
- vows not to use the potion again, after Hyde's behaviour worsens.
- is too weak to stick to his resolution, until Hyde murders Carew.
- changes into Hyde spontaneously, without taking the potion, and has to enlist Lanyon's help to fetch his chemicals. In doing so, he reveals the transformation to Lanyon.
- becomes too afraid to go out in case he suddenly changes into Hyde, which happens increasingly often.
- runs short of a chemical he needs to make his potion and struggles to find more.
- uses the last of the chemical, and writes an account of his history explaining everything to Utterson before he changes to Hyde for the last time.

JEKYLL'S IMPORTANCE TO THE NOVELLA AS A WHOLE

Jekyll is the central **protagonist** of the novella, yet for much of it we see little of him directly. He is introduced by reputation, without being named, as 'the very pink of the proprieties, celebrated too' and 'one of your fellows who do what they call good' (p. 5). Then we hear Lanyon's view of him, as 'too fanciful' and 'wrong, wrong in mind' (p. 9).

For the first eight chapters, we are not aware that Jekyll and Hyde are the same person – this is revealed at the end of Chapter 9. A full account of Jekyll's history and revelation of his character only comes in his own account of events, in Chapter 10. The rest of the novella revolves around him, but as an often shadowy or absent focus.

TOP TIP (A01)

Make sure you are aware of how other characters talk about and interact with Jekyll in the novella, as this is a major source of information about him before his Statement in Chapter 10. What do we learn from his few appearances in the novella before the final chapter?

EXAM FOCUS: WRITING ABOUT JEKYLL

Key point	Evidence/Further meaning
● For a long time, Jekyll has been aware of two aspects of his character in conflict.	● He is aware of 'two natures that contended in the field of [his] consciousness' (p. 58) and 'stood already committed to a profound duplicity of life' (p. 57). ● He leads a double life to appear respectable while satisfying his desires in secret.
● His scientific interests focus on supernatural or spiritual aspects.	● Jekyll says the direction of his scientific studies 'led wholly towards the mystic and transcendental' (p. 58). ● He is concerned with the nature of the soul or personality rather than the physical body.
● As his feeling of duality and his scientific interests come together, he is ambitious and confident in his own intellect.	● 'I began to perceive more deeply than it has ever yet been stated, the trembling immateriality' of the human body (pp. 58–9). ● He sees his discovery as a unique advance in science that no one has approached before.
● He is increasingly tormented by the behaviour of Hyde, becoming reclusive and fearful.	● He will not venture out to walk with Utterson and Enfield (p. 35). ● He is afraid that he will suddenly turn into Hyde – as indeed he does start to do, while they are talking to him through the window.

AIMING HIGH: JEKYLL'S LANGUAGE

For a high level, look at what a character's own words tell us about their personality. The last chapter is told in Jekyll's voice, and it has its own particular style. The richest language in the novella is used by Jekyll in his final statement. Jekyll uses vibrant, flamboyant language, packed with imagery and emotion. He frequently uses similes and metaphors which make his account more vivid.

Jekyll describes phenomena that are completely unfamiliar and impossible to understand. Making comparisons and links with the familiar world helps to explain them. To describe both the closeness and hostility between the parts of his character, he talks about the 'polar twins' of good and evil 'continuously struggling' in the 'agonized womb' of his consciousness (p. 58), or that Hyde 'was knit to him closer than a wife, closer than an eye; lay caged in his flesh' (p. 73). By focusing on familiar aspects of the body – being born, being married, having bodily parts – his words help us to imagine Jekyll's strange experience.

In the end, he feels that language fails him, the uniqueness of his experience defying attempts to explain it: 'It is useless, and the time awfully fails me, to prolong this description; no one has ever suffered such torments, let that suffice' (p. 73).

TOP TIP (A01)

Look out for examples of irony. Jekyll is described by Enfield as: 'an honest man paying through the nose for some of the capers of his youth' (p. 5). Although Enfield is wrong about the blackmail which he supposes Jekyll is suffering, this account of his situation is accurate in ways Enfield cannot know.

TOP TIP: LEARNING ABOUT JEKYLL'S CHARACTER (A01)

We learn about the characters in *Jekyll and Hyde*, as in any piece of fiction, from their actions and words, what other characters say about them, how the narrator presents them, and how other characters behave towards and around them. Make sure you know what Utterson, Lanyon and Poole think of Jekyll. How well does it match the way Jekyll presents himself? Why do they think as they do? Take account of how much they know about Jekyll, remembering that he keeps a lot hidden.

MR EDWARD HYDE

HYDE'S ROLE IN THE NOVELLA

Mr Edward Hyde is the **alter ego** of Jekyll. He does not exist until freed from within Jekyll's psyche by the transformative potion Jekyll takes and drinks. The fullest account of Hyde comes in Jekyll's final statement. We need to put this together with his appearances earlier in the **novella** to see what he does in sequence. In the novella he:

- first emerges when Jekyll first takes his potion.
- is used by Jekyll as a way of enjoying unspecified guilty pleasures in secret.
- tramples a young girl underfoot, which is witnessed by Enfield.
- is forced to pay £100 compensation to the girl's family, and has to draw a cheque on Jekyll's account.
- grows stronger as Jekyll changes into him more frequently.
- murders Carew and is seen doing so.
- begins to emerge without Jekyll taking the potion, which happens increasingly frequently.
- destroys things valued by Jekyll.
- takes cyanide to kill himself (and Jekyll).

HYDE'S IMPORTANCE TO THE NOVELLA AS A WHOLE

Hyde is the evil aspect of Jekyll manifested in a separate identity, and as such forms a part of the main **protagonist**. It is his character and actions that drive Jekyll to his destruction. He is also responsible for all the main events of the novella – the trampling of a young girl recalled by Enfield, the murder of Carew, the death of Lanyon and the destruction of Jekyll.

TOP TIP (A02)

Draw up a timeline of the appearances of Hyde in the first nine chapters of the novella. Using another colour, add in events described by Jekyll in his final statement.

EXAM FOCUS: WRITING ABOUT HYDE

Key point	Evidence/Further meaning
• Everyone finds Hyde immediately repulsive but can't say exactly what is wrong about the way he looks.	• Lanyon says 'there was something abnormal and misbegotten in the very essence of the creature' (p. 53). • His evil and unnaturalness make him look repulsive.
• Only Jekyll does not find Hyde instantly repellent.	• On seeing Hyde in the mirror the first time, Jekyll says, 'I was conscious of no repugnance, rather of a leap of welcome' (p. 61). • Because Hyde is a familiar part of himself, he does not find him repellent.
• Hyde is a distillation of the evil and selfishness in Jekyll.	• Jekyll says he 'was a being inherently malign and villainous; his every act and thought centered on self' (p. 63). • It is his lack of concern for anyone else that makes Hyde especially evil.
• Jekyll often uses imagery relating to the Devil and to animals to talk about Hyde.	• 'My devil had been long caged, he came out roaring' (p. 67). • Devils and animals are clearly distinct from humans, so these images stress how inhuman Hyde is. But animals are part of nature, so at the same time the images acknowledge that the passions Hyde acts on are a natural, if lower, part of us.

AIMING HIGH: HYDE'S APPEARANCE

Hyde looks different from Jekyll. He is shorter, so that Jekyll's clothes hang off his body, looking ridiculous. His hands are darker, smaller and hairier than Jekyll's, with knotted tendons making them look lumpy. In a passage that is difficult to understand, Jekyll explains why his physical appearance changes. He 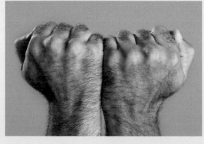 says that the natural body is 'the mere aura and effulgence of certain of the powers that made up my spirit' (p. 59). By this he means that something leaks out of the spirit to shape the physical body, so that a bad person looks ugly and a good person looks pleasant. This was a common idea in the nineteenth century.

MR GABRIEL JOHN UTTERSON

UTTERSON'S ROLE IN THE NOVELLA

Mr Gabriel John Utterson is a lawyer and friend of both Jekyll and Lanyon. We see much of the action of the novella from his point of view, learning things as he learns them. In the novella he:

- hears of Hyde from Enfield, and recognises the name as that of the person favoured in Jekyll's will (which he keeps).
- watches the door until he meets Hyde.
- tries (and fails) to persuade Jekyll to discuss or change his will.
- discovers the rift between Jekyll and Lanyon, but not its cause.
- takes the police inspector Newcomen to Hyde's lodging after the murder of Carew.
- watches the decline of both Lanyon and Jekyll, without knowing the cause.
- goes with Poole to break into the cabinet when Poole fears Jekyll has been murdered.
- reads the documents which explain the whole of the narrative.

UTTERSON'S IMPORTANCE TO THE NOVELLA AS A WHOLE

Utterson is a key character in the novella as he provides continuity and a solid focus during the first eight chapters as events unfurl. His reliable, rational character makes him a good choice as our guide through a story in which events are inexplicable and beyond reason. But he jumps to wrong conclusions about what is happening, and as we take him as our guide we are likely to accept these. This increases the impact of the final revelations.

TOP TIP (A02)

As a lawyer, Utterson is charged with looking after Jekyll's will and it is because of the will that he becomes interested in the character of Hyde. It is also because he is a lawyer that both Lanyon and Utterson leave documents for him to read after Jekyll's death or disappearance. Remember that he is considered to be a reliable, impartial person who will be a good witness to what has happened.

EXAM FOCUS: WRITING ABOUT UTTERSON

Key point	Evidence/Further meaning
● Utterson is a quiet man who builds up friendships slowly and indiscriminately.	● 'his affections, like ivy, were the growth of time, they implied no aptness in the object' (p. 1). ● This means that he does not choose friends carefully, but becomes attached to people who are around for a long time.
● He tends to jump to conclusions and then act as though his assumptions are the certain truth.	● '"Henry Jekyll forge for a murderer!" And his blood ran cold in his veins' (p. 29). ● Utterson interprets the similarity of the handwriting in Hyde's note and Jekyll's note as evidence that Jekyll forged the note on Hyde's behalf.
● He is decisive, keeps his feet on the ground and acts rationally.	● '"Pull yourself together, Bradshaw," said the lawyer. "This suspense, I know, is telling upon all of you; but it is now our intention to make an end of it"' (pp. 42–3). ● Utterson is the figure in authority on the last night, and acts with determination.

AIMING HIGH: STEVENSON AND THE LAW

Stevenson had trained as a lawyer himself, though he did not go on to practise law. This gave him a good insight into the profession, making him well placed to develop Utterson as a character. The first description of Utterson might indicate why Stevenson thought himself not suited to law – perhaps he did not want to be like this himself. Utterson has a 'rugged countenance, that was never lighted by a smile' (p. 1), and is 'backward in sentiment; lean, long, dusty, dreary' (p. 1).

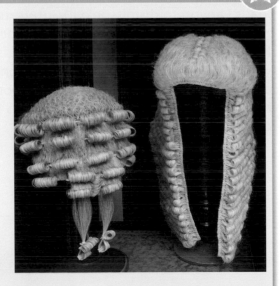

DR HASTIE LANYON

LANYON'S ROLE IN THE NOVELLA

Dr Hastie Lanyon is a medical doctor and an established colleague of Jekyll. However, the two have fallen out and are no longer good friends. In the novella he:

- explains to Utterson that he disagrees with Jekyll's approach to science.
- collects Jekyll's chemicals from his cabinet and takes them to his own rooms, then gives them to Hyde when he arrives.
- suffers the terrible shock of seeing Hyde transform into Jekyll, which leads to his illness and death.
- tells Utterson that the rift between himself and Jekyll has become so deep that they will never meet again.
- writes a letter to Utterson describing the night on which he collected the chemicals and witnessed the transformation.

TOP TIP (A02)

Make sure that you are aware of all Lanyon's appearances and what he does each time he appears in the novella. Draw up a timeline so that you can put the events in order. Remember that the night of the transformation comes before his final meeting with Utterson, even though it is described after this last meeting.

LANYON'S IMPORTANCE IN THE NOVELLA AS A WHOLE

Lanyon is a counterpoint to Jekyll in that his approach to science is entirely practical and based on the physical body, while Jekyll's approach is, in his own words, 'mystic and transcendental' (p. 58). This difference of opinion leads Lanyon to dismiss Jekyll's interests as 'unscientific balderdash' (p. 10). His commitment to his version of science leads him to choose to witness Hyde taking the potion, and also leads to his death as he cannot cope with what he has seen. He is the only person to witness the transformation. His account is essential to the novella in confirming that it does actually happen and is not a figment of Jekyll's imagination, as we might otherwise suppose.

EXAM FOCUS: WRITING ABOUT LANYON

Key point	Evidence/Further meaning
• Lanyon considers that Jekyll's scientific interests are a sign of madness.	• 'it is more than ten years since Henry Jekyll became too fanciful for me. He began to go wrong, wrong in mind' (p. 9). • For Lanyon, science is a purely rational pursuit in which 'fanciful' ideas about the spirit play no part.
• Lanyon's own view of science is thoroughly pragmatic and rational.	• Hyde says Lanyon has been 'bound to the most narrow and material views' (p. 55). • Lanyon will not consider anything that can't be explained in terms of the physical world.
• The challenge to his way of thinking that Hyde's transformation presents is too great for him to bear.	• 'My life is shaken to its roots' (p. 56). • Seeing something completely inexplicable leaves him with no sense of certainty in his life.
• The unleashed evil he has seen in Hyde has filled him with horror that he cannot bear to contemplate.	• 'the moral turpitude that man unveiled to me, even with tears of penitence, I cannot, even in memory, dwell on it without a start of horror' (p. 56). • He is horrified at what he has seen and at what it means.

AIMING HIGH: LANYON'S LANGUAGE

Unlike Jekyll's extravagant language, Lanyon's language is precise and down-to-earth. He uses very little imagery, and tries to give as clear and accurate an account as possible of what he witnesses. He describes the precise changes in the potion Hyde has mixed, and in Hyde's face as he is transformed. The only simile he uses is 'like a man restored from death' (p. 56) when speaking of Jekyll's appearance immediately after the transformation.

MR RICHARD ENFIELD

ENFIELD'S ROLE IN THE NOVELLA

Mr Richard Enfield is a friend and distant cousin of Utterson's. He appears only twice in the novella, when he:

- tells Utterson about Hyde, arousing his curiosity and suspicions.
- suggests that Hyde might be blackmailing Jekyll, an idea Utterson accepts and acts on.
- is walking with Utterson when they try to engage Jekyll in conversation through his window, and they both turn away in horror at the look on Jekyll's face.

EXAM FOCUS: WRITING ABOUT ENFIELD

Key point	Evidence/Further meaning
He is important mainly for describing the episode of Hyde's trampling of a girl.	- The long account is his only substantial speech. - His role is structural rather than as a developed character.
He is a man of action, decisive, pre-emptive and strong.	- 'I gave a view halloa, took to my heels, collared my gentleman, and brought him back' (p. 3). - He pursues Hyde and challenges him, brings him to face the trampled girl's family and extracts money from him.
He usually prefers to keep his views to himself and stay out of other people's business.	- He says he doesn't like to ask questions, and he regrets his 'long tongue' (p. 7) – telling Utterson about the episode involving Hyde. - His preference for keeping to himself provides a reason for him having no further long speeches or opinions in the novella.

TOP TIP (A02)

Enfield is important in the novella because he gives the first impression of Hyde. How far does this shape our view and expectations? Write a description of Hyde from Enfield's account and decide how our view of him changes during the novella.

AIMING HIGH: ASKING QUESTIONS

Look out for clues as to how events might be interpreted. Enfield says that he doesn't like to ask questions because 'You start a question, and it's like starting a stone'. He goes on to say that this stone will pick up others as it rolls down the hill, and 'presently some bland old bird (the last you would have thought of) is knocked on the head in his own back garden and the family have to change their name' (pp. 5–6). Although it looks like a throwaway remark, this is exactly what happens in the case of Jekyll. Not only do others (mostly Utterson) ask questions that snowball, but in asking questions himself Jekyll has set a stone rolling that eventually causes his own destruction. Jekyll is 'the last you would have thought of' to be in such trouble – and he even has to change his name (to Hyde).

POOLE

POOLE'S ROLE IN THE NOVELLA

Poole is Jekyll's butler. He is the most senior of Jekyll's servants, and is the one who interacts with Utterson. In the novella he:

● gives information about Hyde being allowed into Jekyll's laboratory, and a little of his comings and goings.

● tells Utterson when Jekyll will not see him, giving some information about Jekyll's seclusion and state of health.

● comes to fetch Utterson when he thinks Jekyll has been murdered.

● goes with Utterson to break down the door to the cabinet and find Hyde's body.

EXAM FOCUS: WRITING ABOUT POOLE (A01)

Key point	Evidence/Further meaning
● His role as a servant makes him socially inferior to the main characters.	● '"Now, my good man," said the lawyer, "be explicit. What are you afraid of?"' (p. 36). ● Utterson treats him like a servant, challenging him about the opened note to the pharmacist, speaking down to him and giving him instructions
● His style of speech is typical of working-class people at the time.	● 'I don't rightly know how to say it, sir, beyond this: that you felt it in your marrow, kind of cold and thin' (p. 42). ● 'rightly know' and 'kind of' convey the struggle he has to identify and say what he feels.
● He knows Jekyll very well, having worked for him for a long time.	● 'do you think I do not know my master after twenty years?' (p. 41). ● His familiarity with Jekyll's walk, voice and height are key to Utterson deciding to break down the door and expecting to find Hyde.

TOP TIP: WRITING ABOUT POOLE'S FAITHFULNESS (A02)

Poole is faithful to Jekyll, being discreet about his business until his worries lead him to ask Utterson for help. Poole helps Lanyon to fetch the drawer of chemicals from the cabinet, not apparently questioning Jekyll's strange request, and observes his wishes to be left in peace. He tries to obtain the chemicals Jekyll wants, and leaves him food on the stairs to take into his cabinet. He only breaks trust when he fears Jekyll is in danger, or already murdered: 'I think there's been foul play' (p. 36).

INSPECTOR NEWCOMEN

NEWCOMEN'S ROLE IN THE NOVELLA

Inspector Newcomen is the police officer involved in trying to solve the Carew murder case. In the novella he:

- takes the letter Carew is carrying to Utterson.
- hears Utterson identify Carew.
- goes with Utterson to Hyde's lodgings.
- leads the investigation into the murder.

EXAM FOCUS: WRITING ABOUT NEWCOMEN

Key point	Evidence/Further meaning
• He is ambitious and wants to solve the case of Carew's murder.	• 'his eye lighted up with professional ambition' (p. 21). • Newcomen is not touched emotionally by the case – he sees it purely as a professional challenge.
• We only know the Inspector's name because Utterson introduces him to Hyde's landlady.	• In order to persuade the landlady to show them the room, Utterson names the Inspector; he is not given a first name. • He is not important as a character in his own right, only in his role as the investigating police officer.

TOP TIP: WRITING ABOUT NEWCOMEN'S DETACHMENT

A02

Notice how the Inspector is pleased by each discovery that helps him towards solving the case. He is 'delighted' (p. 24) to find the broken walking stick, evidence that Hyde killed Carew, and finding a lot of money is in Hyde's bank account 'completed his gratification' (p. 24). When his eyes light up at learning Carew's identity, it is because the murder of a 'Sir' and MP will be a high-profile case, and good for his career if he is associated with a successful outcome.

SIR DANVERS CAREW AND MR GUEST

CAREW'S ROLE IN THE NOVELLA

Sir Danvers Carew is murdered by Hyde in a brutal, unprovoked attack. We hear about him through the testament of the maid who witnessed the attack. He is acknowledged to be a friend and client of Utterson.

EXAM FOCUS: WRITING ABOUT CAREW

Key point	Evidence/Further meaning
• He is an elegant, sophisticated elderly man, still sprightly enough to walk alone late at night.	• The maid describes him as 'an aged and beautiful gentleman, with white hair' (p. 20). • This tells us he is respectable and not doing anything that might annoy Hyde.
• He is of high social standing.	• His title is 'Sir', he carries a purse and a gold watch, and the newsboy's cry tells us he was an MP. • His high profile and social position would have made the murder and more pressing for the police.

GUEST'S ROLE IN THE NOVELLA

Mr Guest is Utterson's chief clerk and an expert in reading someone's character from their handwriting (graphology) – he identifies a crucial similarity between Jekyll's handwriting and that in a note from Hyde.

EXAM FOCUS: WRITING ABOUT GUEST

Key point	Evidence/Further meaning
• Utterson appears to trust Guest, which speaks well of his character.	• 'There was no man from whom he kept fewer secrets than Mr Guest' (p. 28). • Utterson needs to share confidential information with Guest and so trusts him absolutely.
• Utterson expects Guest to speak if he spots anything odd in Hyde's handwriting.	• 'he would scarce read so strange a document without dropping a remark' (p. 28).
• Guest decides the writer of the note is not mentally unstable.	• Utterson says 'The man, of course, was mad' (p. 28), but Guest disagrees: 'not mad; but it is an odd hand' (p. 29). • This is important when we later discover Hyde and Jekyll are the same person, as Jekyll does not seem unstable.

THE MAID AND HYDE'S LANDLADY

THE MAID'S ROLE IN THE NOVELLA

The maid appears only once, when the murder of Carew is told from her point of view. She watches from her window as Carew walks down the road, encounters Hyde and is violently murdered. She faints, which gives Hyde time to get away, and later alerts the police.

EXAM FOCUS: WRITING ABOUT THE MAID

Key point	Evidence/Further meaning
• The maid gives a romanticised account of Carew.	• She says the man 'seemed to breathe such an innocent and old-world kindness of disposition, yet with something high too, as of a well-founded self-content' (p. 20). • She does not know Carew, and is making assumptions about his character from his appearance.
• The account of Carew is given partly in words that could be the maid's, even though it is not a first-person narrative.	• 'the moon shone on his face as he spoke, and the girl was pleased to watch it' (p. 20). • This invites us to imagine the maid giving her evidence, saying she watched because the scene was attractive.

THE LANDLADY'S ROLE IN THE NOVELLA

The landlady is seen only when Utterson and Newcomen visit Hyde's lodgings. She gives them information about Hyde's coming and going and shows them his room. She seems pleased that Hyde is in trouble.

EXAM FOCUS: WRITING ABOUT THE LANDLADY

Key point	Evidence/Further meaning
• The landlady is polite, but unpleasant.	• She had an evil face, smoothed by hypocrisy; but her manners were excellent' (p. 23). • Her ill-feeling is hidden by politeness, making her a hypocrite.
• She is indiscreet in telling Utterson and Newcomen about Hyde before knowing who they are.	• She tells them his 'habits were very irregular' (p. 23) and that he had been away for two months. • She is a gossip, and abuses her knowledge as a landlady.
• She is pleased that Hyde is in trouble.	• 'A flash of odious joy appeared upon the woman's face' (p. 23). • Her pleasure suggests she too feels the revulsion Hyde arouses.

PROGRESS AND REVISION CHECK

SECTION ONE: CHECK YOUR KNOWLEDGE

1. How does Utterson choose and treat his friends?

2. What it is it about Hyde that everyone first notices?

3. What drives Jekyll to make and experiment with his potion?

4. Why do Jekyll and Lanyon disagree?

5. What makes Poole share confidential details about Jekyll with Utterson?

6. What is Carew like, according to the maid?

7. Why does Jekyll become afraid to go out or receive visitors?

8. Why do we follow Utterson's lead when he jumps to conclusions or makes assumptions?

9. Which aspect of the presentation of Poole shows his social status?

10. Which characteristic of Inspector Newcomen comes across in his pursuit of Hyde?

TOP TIP (A01)

Answer these quick questions to test your knowledge of the characters.

SECTION TWO: CHECK YOUR UNDERSTANDING

Task: What role does curiosity or lack of it play in the characters in *The Strange Case of Dr Jekyll and Mr Hyde*? Think about:

● which characters display curiosity, or lack of it

● the effect on the narrative of characters' curiosity, or lack of it.

TOP TIP (A01)

This task requires a slightly longer response. Try to write at least three to four paragraphs.

PROGRESS CHECK

GOOD PROGRESS

I can:

● explain the significance of the main characters in how the action develops. ☐

● refer to how they are described by Stevenson and how this affects the way we see them. ☐

EXCELLENT PROGRESS

I can:

● analyse in detail how Stevenson has shaped and developed characters over the course of the novella. ☐

● infer key ideas, themes and issues from the ways characters and relationships are presented by Stevenson. ☐

THEMES

DUALITY

The plot of *Jekyll and Hyde* hinges on the dual nature of human beings. Stevenson suggests that we have both:

- a base part concerned with physical appetites and pleasures, and
- a higher part that is concerned with intellectual pleasures, moral behaviour and the life of the mind.

Jekyll feels a terrible tension between how he instinctively wants to behave and how he feels he should behave in order to be well regarded in society. This dual nature that he feels in himself leads him to try to separate the two parts into two different beings.

The duality of human natures is not the only type of duality the novella deals with. There are others, which form themes of their own, including:

- good and evil
- science and the supernatural
- appearance and reality.

THE DUALITY OF HUMAN NATURE

The most important duality Stevenson presents in the novella is his idea of the dual aspect of human nature: the noble part that follows the conscience and the selfish part that is interested only in pleasure-seeking. This duality is presented through Jekyll who:

- sees it as natural, recognising the 'thorough and primitive duality of man' (p. 58).
- believes it is a source of trouble and misery that 'lies at the root of religion and is one of the most plentiful springs of distress' (p. 57).
- makes a doomed attempt to separate the two parts of himself, which can only fail because 'This, too, was myself' (p. 61).
- recognises the two parts 'divide and compound' (p. 57) human nature.
- suggests that human nature might not just be dual, but multiple: a 'polity of multifarious, incongruent and independent denizens' (p. 58).

AIMING HIGH: BODY AND SOUL

The conflict between body and soul was familiar to Stevenson and his readers from Christian tradition and a long tradition of Western philosophy stretching back to the Ancient Greeks. The image of the noble soul struggling to escape the degrading passions of the body is a familiar motif in Christianity. Ancient Greek philosophers such as Aristotle and Plato also discussed the separation of the body into base instincts – the 'lower elements in my soul' (p. 59) as Jekyll calls them – and the higher intellect. Plato described a person's rational faculty as being like a charioteer trying to steer a reasonable course, with these two impulses as horses pulling in opposite directions.

TOP TIP (A02)

Look out, too, for smaller hints at duality, such as the two aspects of Jekyll's house (the smart façade facing the street, and the shabby back door that Hyde uses).

THEME TRACKER (A01)

The duality of human nature

- Ch. 6 p. 30: Jekyll is one day sociable and the next day shut away and refusing to see anyone.

- Ch. 10 p. 57: Jekyll describes how he felt he was two people in one body.

- Ch. 10 p. 60: Jekyll first releases his alter ego, Hyde.

GOOD AND EVIL

The theme of good and evil is closely linked with that of the duality of human nature. Evil is personified in Hyde:

- Jekyll says Hyde is 'alone in the ranks of mankind, pure evil' (p. 61).
- His evil lies in being entirely selfish: he will do whatever he wants to satisfy his own appetites without any regard for other people.

Good, on the other hand, is shown in the novella as being generous and kind to others:

- Enfield describes Jekyll as 'one of your fellows who do what they call good' (p. 5).
- When freed from his bad aspects, Jekyll works for charities, is religious, is a good friend and 'he did good' (p. 30).

Hyde's acts of violence and destruction are contrasted with the goodness of their subjects:

- the innocent small girl
- Carew, who has 'an innocent and old-world kindness' about him (p. 20)
- the devotional book that Hyde defaces.

AIMING HIGH: WRITING ABOUT THE NATURE OF EVIL ⭐

As in many works of literature that deal with good and evil, there is more about evil in *Jekyll and Hyde* than there is about good. Make sure you keep track of instances when the good nature of characters – particularly Jekyll – is shown. Jekyll says that even though Hyde is purely evil, Jekyll is still a mix, though his worst instincts have been moved into Hyde. What does this say about the nature of good? Many aspects that we consider 'good' are defined in relation to what is bad, which makes it hard to think about goodness on its own.

FRIENDSHIP

Friendship is a minor theme in the novella. There are several pairs of friends:

- Enfield and Utterson are friends, though 'It was a nut to crack for many, what these two could see in each other' (p. 2).
- Utterson, Lanyon and Jekyll are friends who dine together.
- Jekyll and Lanyon are long-standing professional friends, though they fall out over Jekyll's approach to science.

Friendship is also a spur to the action:

- Utterson's friendship with Jekyll leads him to investigate Hyde and to become involved in the action of the story.
- Poole asks Utterson, as Jekyll's friend, to help him on the final night.
- Jekyll turns to Lanyon as one of his 'oldest friends' (p. 49) when he needs chemicals from his cabinet.

The novella looks at how and why people make and break friendships, and what obligations friendship places on people.

THEME TRACKER A01

Good and evil

- Ch. 1 p. 3: Hyde tramples a small child.
- Ch. 1 p. 20: Hyde murders Carew.
- Ch. 10 p. 61: Jekyll talks about the evil of Hyde.

THEME TRACKER (A01)

Science

● Ch. 2 pp. 9–10: Lanyon explains the difference in his approach to science and Jekyll's approach.

● Ch. 9 pp. 54–6: Lanyon describes the physical changes in the potion and in Hyde.

● Ch. 10 pp. 61–2: Jekyll describes taking his potion and the effects it had.

SCIENCE

Science is a major theme in the **novella**. There are two principal views of science:

● Lanyon follows a practical, rational type of science, described by Hyde as showing 'narrow and material views' (p. 55).

● Jekyll has a more mystical and supernatural – or 'transcendental' (p. 55) – approach, which Lanyon considers 'unscientific balderdash' (p. 10) and 'scientific heresies' (p. 17).

These different approaches lead to different styles of descriptive language. Lanyon's account gives as much clear, factual detail as possible, describing:

● the effect on himself of seeing Hyde

● the appearance of the chemicals before and after mixing

● the physical symptoms he observed in Hyde as he changed.

But the transformation is so bizarre that normal science and its language cannot adequately account for or describe it. Jekyll describes his experience in much more abstract, poetic language that does not communicate scientific facts:

● He speaks of 'the trembling immateriality, the mist-like transience' (p. 59) of the physical body.

● He says the potion 'shook the very fortress of identity' (p. 59).

KEY QUOTATION: SCIENCE DOES NOT DISCRIMINATE (A01)

In his Statement, Jekyll is careful to point out that it is not the potion itself that causes good or evil: 'The drug had no discriminating action; it was neither diabolical nor divine; it but shook the doors of the prisonhouse of my disposition' (p. 61).

This helps to align him with a more rigorous scientific approach. He means that the effect the potion has on the person who takes it depends on the state of that person – it is just a reaction to a chemical.

APPEARANCE AND REALITY

Few things are as they seem in the novella. For example:

● Jekyll is considered a respectable, upstanding man, but feels he hides a dark inner identity

● Hyde appears to be a normal, if ugly, person but is actually a 'child of Hell' (p. 71)

● Jekyll's predicament: it looks as though he is being blackmailed, and this is what Enfield and Utterson assume is happening

● the physical deterioration of Lanyon looks to Utterson like a physical illness, but is the result of the shock of seeing Hyde's transformation

● Utterson assumes Jekyll's odd behaviour means that he is ill and seeking a cure.

We as readers are also taken in by these deceptive appearances.

CONTEXTS

STEVENSON'S LIFE

The author was born Robert Lewis Balfour Stevenson, in Edinburgh in 1850 (he later changed the spelling of his first middle name to Louis and dropped the second one).

- Edinburgh had a very famous medical school, and the doctors trained there were generally considered the best in Britain. Stevenson would have been familiar with this reputation; the 'Sawbones' who attends the trampled girl has 'a strong Edinburgh accent' (p. 4).

- His father wanted Stevenson to train as an engineer, but Stevenson switched to law at university. This gave him a good background on which to draw when creating the character of Utterson and dealing with the law as a theme in *Jekyll and Hyde*. Stevenson never practised law, deciding to become a writer instead.

- Stevenson gave up religion and became an atheist, quarrelling with his father as a result. Although *Jekyll and Hyde* is not specifically anti-Christian, it deals with issues that are problematic within the Christian Church, such as the nature of evil and why people have urges to do bad things.

Robert Louis Stevenson

VICTORIAN LONDON

Victorian London was a dramatic place, used extensively as a setting for fiction both at the time and since. Stevenson draws on two well-known features of London:

- There were rich people, but there were also very poor people, living in overcrowded and squalid conditions. Stevenson draws on the extremes, with Lanyon's house and Jekyll's house both being in respectable areas, but the rooms Jekyll has rented for Hyde being in a poor neighbourhood.

- London was subject to very thick, dark fog which rose from the River Thames and mixed with soot and smoke in the atmosphere from the many coal fires burning in the city. Sometimes, it was impossible for people to see their hand in front of their face. Stevenson uses the fog to create a gloomy, dark atmosphere. The fog could even creep inside buildings, as it does in Jekyll's cabinet.

REVISION FOCUS: THE WEATHER

Pay attention to the weather in *Jekyll and Hyde*. It is not always foggy. Go through the novella and make sure that you notice whenever Stevenson mentions the weather, and note down what it adds to each scene. Are more cheerful scenes marked by brighter weather? Linking the weather to the temperaments of the characters or the type of activity going on is a common feature in many novels.

TOP TIP (A03)

It can be useful to watch films of a book you are studying to see the setting and costumes. But remember that most films of novels change the story and the characters a lot. Films of *Jekyll and Hyde* will show you the London of Stevenson's day, but the plots rarely follow the novella so a film won't help with your revision.

SCIENCE

Great advances in science in the nineteenth century changed the way that people thought about the world and about the nature of human beings. These are reflected in *Jekyll and Hyde* in several ways:

- Darwin's theory of **evolution** (published in 1859) stated that humans had evolved from other animals and were not, as the Bible teaches, unique and specially created by God. The idea that humans were a type of animal was very difficult for many people to accept, and challenged their view of what it is to be human. Stevenson draws on this uncertainty about the nature of humankind.

- Advances in chemistry and biology looked at how the body works and how chemicals work, and work on us. **Pharmacology**, which studies how chemicals act on the body, emerged as a major new science in the mid-nineteenth century. Jekyll's development of his potion is an exercise in pharmacology.

- **Psychology** emerged as a science in the 1880s. It explores the working of the mind and how it interacts with the body – areas that interest Jekyll.

- **Graphology** was a popular pseudo-science (not a 'real' science) in the nineteenth century. It claims to reveal features of personality from someone's handwriting. Stevenson uses it to show that Jekyll is 'not mad' (p. 29) and that his handwriting is very similar to Hyde's.

- **Physiognomy** was another pseudo-science. It suggests that we can learn about someone's character from what they look like. Stevenson uses this idea in making Hyde physically repulsive, with his evil shown in his appearance.

AIMING HIGH: READING FACES

Make sure you can relate the treatment of science in the book to contemporary Victorian approaches to science. Physiognomy had been popularised in the eighteenth century by Johann Kaspar Lavater in Switzerland. He believed that 'an exact relationship exists between the soul and the body'. Jekyll voices a similar idea when he says that his body is 'the mere aura and effulgence of certain of the powers that made up my spirit' (p. 59).

TOP TIP

Consider whether you think the novella might suggest a rejection of science: it has not served either Lanyon or Jekyll well. Stevenson himself rejected the science of engineering, which his father wanted him to study, so perhaps he was thinking about the limitations of science.

THE LAW

The law provides another context within which the story is set.

- Utterson is a lawyer, and keeps the legal documents involved in documenting the case as well as keeping Jekyll's will. It was the will which first aroused Utterson's suspicions and interest.
- Important parts of the story are recorded in formal, legal documents, which generally record the truth: Lanyon's witness account and Jekyll's statement both give the story an aura of authenticity.
- Newcomen represents another aspect of the law, but one which is ultimately unsuccessful in dealing with such strange events.

GOTHIC LITERATURE

The Strange Case of Dr Jekyll and Mr Hyde is written in the tradition of **Gothic** literature. This began in the eighteenth century and was popular throughout the nineteenth century.

- Gothic novels deal with human experience on the margins of normality. They deal with horror, madness and extremes of emotion such as despair and great passion. *Jekyll and Hyde* clearly falls within this tradition. Jekyll and Lanyon are driven mad with despair and horror at what Jekyll has done.
- Most Gothic literature has supernatural elements, such as ghosts or psychic experiences. The separation of parts of Jekyll's personality is achieved through a supernatural – or at least paranormal – transformation.
- Gothic settings are dark and mysterious, often with ornate architecture, such as castles and towers, and dark forests. Although Stevenson sets his novella in London, the perpetual fog and darkness, and his account of a 'district of some city in a nightmare' (p. 22), create a Gothic atmosphere.

AIMING HIGH: GOTHIC NOVELS

You need to be able to place the **novella** in literary tradition. The most famous British Gothic novels are *Frankenstein*, written in 1816 by Mary Shelley, and *Dracula*, written by Bram Stoker in 1897 – after *Jekyll and Hyde*. Another important Gothic writer is the American short-story writer Edgar Allan Poe. *Jane Eyre* by Charlotte Brontë and *Wuthering Heights* by Emily Brontë (both published in 1847), and many of Charles Dickens's novels, also share in the Gothic tradition. Stevenson would have been aware of all of these except *Dracula*.

KEY CONTEXT (A03)

As Stevenson had trained as a lawyer, he would have been familiar with the format required for a will and a formal statement. He would also have been aware that it is fruitless to try to apply rigorous disciplines such as the law and science to a case as 'fanciful' (p. 9) as this. The law tries to make order and structure out of the chaos of people's behaviour, but the novella does not show it succeeding.

KEY CONTEXT (A03)

Oscar Wilde's Gothic novel, *The Picture of Dorian Gray* (1891) was published five years after *Jekyll and Hyde* and also features a central character with a split-personality. After seeing a portrait of himself, Dorian vows that he would give his soul if the picture could age while he remains young. Dorian gets his wish but he is corrupted by the deal he has made and while he stays beautiful on the outside his wicked soul is reflected in the painting, which becomes monstrously ugly.

SETTINGS

INSIDE SETTINGS

The interior locations where action is set are:

- Jekyll's house and cabinet: these reflect the dual aspect of Jekyll/Hyde. The hall is 'the pleasantest room in London' (p. 14), yet it is connected to the laboratory that has a sinister history as a dissecting room. Above that is Jekyll's cabinet, where he carries out his experiments. It appears pleasant, with a fire and tea things laid out, 'the quietest room, you would have said' (p. 44). There are corridors and a cellar 'filled with crazy lumber' (p. 45) that had belonged to the surgeon who lived there previously.

- Utterson's house: this is not well described. We learn only that he sits in a chair by the fire, near his reading desk, and that in his 'business room' (p. 8) there is a safe in which he keeps important documents such as Jekyll's will.

- Lanyon's house: there is no description of Lanyon's house beyond its being in Cavendish Square, a smart area of London and 'citadel of medicine' (p. 9) at the time. Lanyon lives in the building where he receives his patients.

- Hyde's lodgings: these also combine pleasant and unpleasant aspects. The lodgings are in 'blackguardly surroundings' (p. 23) but are 'furnished with luxury and good taste' (p. 23). There are fine silverware, good carpets and a painting on the wall, yet the rooms have been ransacked and are in a state of chaos.

AIMING HIGH: SETTING AND STATES OF MIND

Make sure you are aware how Stevenson's settings can reflect the internal state of a character. Hyde's lodgings are 'furnished with luxury and good taste', but 'bore every mark of having been recently and hurriedly ransacked' (p. 23). This reflects the state of Jekyll's mind: he is a cultured man, yet at the same time plunged into chaos, distraught and confused. Sometimes events contrast strongly with setting. Poole and Utterson break into the cabinet to find a pleasant setting: 'a good fire glowing and chattering on the hearth, the kettle singing'. But in the midst of this is 'the body of a man sorely contorted and still twitching' (p. 44). The presence of the corpse in a domestic setting is shocking – especially so because the cosy description encourages us to relax after the tension of previous events.

OUTDOOR SETTINGS

Outdoor activity consists mostly of journeys. Generally, the settings and incidents outside are grim. Jekyll's house has a respectable aspect on one street, but the dingy, peeling door near the courtyard that Hyde uses on another. The two aspects of the house recall the two aspects of Jekyll. Utterson's trip with Newcomen to Hyde's lodgings is through a grim cityscape, only occasionally visible through the fog. The two attacks in the street made by Hyde take place at night, while Utterson travels at night with Poole to Jekyll's house when Poole thinks Jekyll has been murdered. The outdoor setting in London's darkness and fog adds to the Gothic atmosphere of the novella.

Dr Jekyll's house – front   Dr Jekyll's house – back

Mr Utterson's house

Dr Lanyon's house

Mr Hyde's lodgings

PROGRESS AND REVISION CHECK

SECTION ONE: CHECK YOUR KNOWLEDGE

1 Which two characters are most closely associated with the theme of science?

2 How does Jekyll's house reflect his split personality?

3 Give two elements of *The Strange Case of Dr Jekyll and Mr Hyde* that are related to the Gothic theme.

4 Why is it often foggy in the novella?

5 Which aspect of Stevenson's own life prepared him to write about Utterson?

6 Which writer of detective fiction was writing at the same time as Stevenson?

7 Which character tries always to give a clear, detailed account even of horrifying events?

8 Which character's voice is marked by complex, carefully constructed questions?

9 Enfield refers to the Harpies; which type of literary device is this?

10 Which characters act as first-person narrators in the novella?

SECTION TWO: CHECK YOUR UNDERSTANDING

Task: Consider the presentation of science in *The Strange Case of Jekyll and Mr Hyde.* How does Stevenson use his characters to put forward different aspects? Think about how science is portrayed through:

● Jekyll

● Lanyon.

PROGRESS CHECK

GOOD PROGRESS

I can:

● explain the main themes, contexts and settings in the novella and how they contribute to the effect on the reader. ☐

● use a range of appropriate evidence to support any points I make about these elements. ☐

EXCELLENT PROGRESS

I can:

● analyse in detail the way themes are developed and presented across the novella. ☐

● refer closely to key aspects of context and setting and the implications they have for the writer's viewpoint, and the interpretation of relationships and ideas. ☐

FORM

THE NOVELLA

Jekyll and Hyde is a **novella**. This means that it is shorter than a regular novel, but longer and with a more complicated structure than a short story.

THE GOTHIC NOVEL

Jekyll and Hyde is an example of **Gothic** literature. Gothic novels first appeared in the eighteenth century.

- Most were long, rambling narratives with many episodes and often involving journeys.
- *Jekyll and Hyde* is shorter than other Gothic novels and it is set entirely in London.
- All deal with extremes of emotion, madness, and with horrifying, violent and supernatural events.
- Gothic novels often use **interpolated narratives** in spoken accounts, letters, diaries and other documents to help tell the story. They allow the author to tell parts of the story from different characters' points of view, keeping other parts hidden.
- Stevenson uses this technique to maintain the mystery while telling the story, then to show the intense emotions of Lanyon and Jekyll in their accounts.

THE DETECTIVE NOVEL

The detective story was a new form in the nineteenth century. It was made popular by Arthur Conan Doyle's stories of Sherlock Holmes. *Jekyll and Hyde* borrows from the tradition.

- A detective novel usually starts with a crime – most often a murder – which is then solved, following a trail of false and true leads. In *Jekyll and Hyde* we know the crimes we see are committed by Hyde – there is apparently no need to uncover 'whodunnit'.
- Detective stories often have a twist at the end – the criminal is not who we expected, or the crime was not what it seemed. *Jekyll and Hyde* has a very unusual twist at the end. In the final chapters we learn what really happened, and how and why it happened. The mystery is solved, and we learn that we did not know 'whodunnit' after all: actually it was Jekyll, because he *is* Hyde.

TOP TIP (A01)

The central mystery of *Jekyll and Hyde* is not who committed the crime, but the nature of the relationship between Jekyll and Hyde.

⭐ AIMING HIGH: EXTRA NARRATIVES

Make sure you are aware of all the separate narratives in *Jekyll and Hyde*, including the reports by different characters (such as Enfield's account of Hyde at the start), and the documents reproduced in the text. Letters and diaries are a common feature of Gothic literature, and also of detective or mystery novels. They allow different points of view to be shown, and enable the novelist to present events that the main characters or narrator could not have witnessed.

STRUCTURE

ACTION AND INACTION

We witness very little action in *Jekyll and Hyde*.

- Most vigorous action is not narrated directly. Hyde's attacks are told by Enfield and from the point of view of the maid after the event.
- Much of the novella deals with the aftermath of events, and shows characters talking together or trying to work out what has been happening.
- The only action we witness first-hand is Utterson and Poole breaking down the door to the cabinet. They are too late to witness Hyde's suicide.
- The final two chapters are more immediate, even though the action is in the past. We forget that we are reading a document alongside Utterson, and are caught up in the story as though it were happening before our eyes.
- Because Utterson does not return at the end of the novella, this impression is never disrupted.

REVISION FOCUS: TIMESCALE

Draw up a table that shows what actually happens in real time in each chapter, and which past events are narrated. Use this structure, following the example of the first chapter:

Chapter	Happens	Recounted
Chapter 1	Utterson and Enfield take a walk	Hyde's attack on the young girl

KEY STRUCTURE: TENSION AND SUSPENSE **A02**

Tension in the novella increases along with the sense of mystery. Stevenson handles this by making us curious.

- Our curiosity about what is really happening, and who Hyde is, is bound up with Utterson's curiosity. As he wonders what is happening, and makes conjectures, so we become more interested in the questions that he poses. Stevenson uses him to direct our curiosity.
- The existence of documents which apparently contain the answers to the questions, and which Utterson cannot yet look at, increases the suspense.
- The responses of the characters – the increasing despair and near madness of Jekyll and Lanyon – show that events are certainly of an extreme nature, and make us long to find out what is happening.

LANGUAGE

OVERVIEW

- Robert Louis Stevenson's style can be difficult to read at first. He often uses long sentences and unfamiliar words. He was not being deliberately difficult – it is just that writing styles have changed in the last 150 years.
- Once you get used to his style, you will find that it is dense and rich, with a lot of information and nuance packed in.
- The words are chosen carefully and often have connotations or associations that add an extra dimension to what the text is saying.

LANGUAGE DEVICE: VOICE

What is 'voice'?	The way a character or narrator speaks. This includes the directly spoken words of characters, and the words the narrator uses to relate the action, comment on it or address the reader.
Example	Poole uses simpler language than most of the other characters: 'But if you mean, was it Mr Hyde? – why, yes, I think it was! You see, it was much of the same bigness; and it had the same quick, light way with it' (p. 42).
Effect	This informal language shows Poole is less articulate and well-educated than the main characters.

The characters in *Jekyll and Hyde* have different voices that reflect their personalities and concerns. For example:

- Utterson speaks in measured, formal sentences and never uses a simple word when there is a complicated word that can be used instead. When Poole says he thinks Hyde is in the house, Utterson says, 'My fears incline to the same point' (p. 42), when a simpler way of putting it would be to say, 'I think so, too'. Formal and wordy speech is characteristic of his profession as a lawyer.

- Lanyon speaks very precisely, giving lots of factual detail. He rarely embellishes his speech with imagery or any display of imagination, such as conjecture or supposition. This suits his nature as a rigorously practical scientist.

- Jekyll, on the other hand, speaks in a rich and flamboyant style, often using imagery and words that are emotionally loaded. This suits his more unusual scientific interests.

TOP TIP (A01)

The Inspector's social rank is below that of Utterson, but above that of the landlady. In saying Hyde 'don't seem a very popular character' (p. 23), his grammatically incorrect use of 'don't' and his use of 'character' mark him as less well-educated than Utterson. But he refers to the landlady as 'my good woman' (p. 23), indicating that he is above her socially.

LANGUAGE DEVICE: NARRATORIAL VOICE

What is narratorial voice?	The voice in which the action is related. A narrator can speak in the first person about their own experiences, or in the third person about what happens to other people.
Example	Lanyon and Jekyll are first-person narrators: 'I sought with tears and prayers to smother down the crowd of hideous images and sounds with which my memory swarmed' (p. 68) Jekyll says.
Effect	A first-person narrator can give a very personal and intimate insight, but also limits the narrative to their point of view and what they have seen and done.

Most of *Jekyll and Hyde* is told by a third-person narrator, but from the point of view of Utterson. This means that we learn the story as it is revealed to Utterson, and we don't know things that he does not know. It is not quite the same as having the story told by Utterson, as the narrator can comment on Utterson from the outside – describing him, for example, in words that he might not use himself: 'cold, scanty and embarrassed in discourse; backward in sentiment' (p. 1).

LANGUAGE DEVICE: IMAGERY

Other characters take over as narrator on several occasions, telling the story in the first person. For example, Enfield acts as a first-person narrator to describe the episode in which he first saw Hyde (Chapter 1).

What is imagery?	The use of vivid language that calls up visual (or other sensory or imaginative) comparisons to help us see something in a new way.
Example	Jekyll talks of 'sensual images running like a mill race' in his mind (p. 60). A mill race is the turbulent rush of water at a water mill.
Effect	This image makes us attribute the characteristics of a mill race to the state of his mind – his thoughts are rushing around chaotically.

TOP TIP (A02)

The third-person narrator sometimes adopts the voices of another character to show events from their point of view. For example, when the maid describes Carew's murder, the voice reflects her thoughts about the 'aged and beautiful gentleman' (p. 20).

The different voices in *Jekyll and Hyde* use imagery differently. Jekyll is the character who uses most imagery. He is often trying to communicate complex and unfamiliar ideas, and experiences that no one else has ever had. To make it easier to grasp, he uses images, relating the unknown to things that are familiar. This helps us to approach what he is trying to describe.

Jekyll often uses similes. He uses words such as 'like' and 'as' to show the similarity between two things. He says that the heady feeling he felt on turning into Hyde 'braced and delighted me like wine' (p. 60) – one thing was 'like' another.

He also uses metaphors. A metaphor describes one thing in terms of another as though it actually were the other thing. Jekyll talks of the two aspects of his nature as 'these polar twins' (polar meaning opposite in nature) that are 'continuously struggling' in the 'agonized womb of consciousness' (p. 58). He does not say that the two parts of himself are *like* twins or that it was *as though* his consciousness was a womb – he speaks as if this were actually the case.

TOP TIP (A02)

Jekyll often refers to his physical body, and the form of his alter ego, Hyde, using clothing imagery. Find as many of these images as you can. If the body is like clothing, which can be slipped on and off, what is it that is being clothed?

LANGUAGE DEVICE: SENTENCE STYLE

What is sentence style?	Sentences can be long or short, simple or complex. They can serve different functions: to relate action, ask a question or report speech, for instance.
Example	Utterson often uses complicated structure: 'It is one thing to mortify curiosity, another to conquer it; and it may be doubted if, from that day forth, Utterson desired the society of his surviving friend with the same eagerness' (p. 33).
Effect	This sentence uses grammar with care and precision, suggesting the control and attention to detail characteristic of Utterson.

The long sentences in the novella can be hard to follow. Stevenson often uses subordinate clauses, inserted into a sentence or phrase, such as 'from that day forth' in the example above.

Short, simple sentences are used for impact and to present the thoughts and speech of less-educated characters. Sometimes they are interjections, such as, '"God forgive us, God forgive us," said Mr Utterson' (p. 35).

Sometimes a character's speech shows emotion through disorganised or abrupt structure or rhythm. Lanyon's narrative shows this: 'As for the moral turpitude that man unveiled to me, even with tears of penitence, I cannot, even in memory, dwell on it without a start of horror' (p. 56). The sentence seems broken up and choppy, reflecting his emotional state.

TOP TIP: UNDERSTANDING LONG SENTENCES

- If you have difficulty with a sentence, try first to look for the subject – what it is about – and then find the verb (which tells you what is happening, or what the subject is doing). You can then work out how the other parts of the sentence relate to that main action.

- Stevenson often uses a semicolon (;) to join together two parts that could have been separate sentences. It is easier to treat the parts as sentences in their own right.

- Ignore the extra clauses while working out what is most important.

- Here is an example. The most important phrases are underlined, and the numbers show the different sections of the sentence:

    (1) 'The doctor, it appeared, now more than ever confined himself to the cabinet over the laboratory, where he would sometimes even sleep; (2) he was out of spirits, he had grown very silent, he did not read; (3) it seemed as if he had something on his mind' (p. 32).

LANGUAGE DEVICE: GOTHIC STYLE

KEY CONTEXT **A03**

Arthur Conan Doyle published the first of his Sherlock Holmes stories, 'A Study in Scarlet', in the same year as Stevenson published *Jekyll and Hyde*. Stevenson had already written detective fiction himself, a collection of short stories called *The Suicide Club*, in 1878.

What is Gothic style?	Ornate, intensely rich and dense style that combines imagery, strong emotion and long, complicated sentences.
Example	Jekyll says 'the slime of the pit seemed to utter cries and voices; that the amorphous dust gesticulated and sinned' (p. 73).
Effect	The horrifying images create a sense of revulsion and terror that helps us to imagine Jekyll's feelings.

There is no moderation in Gothic style – it uses horror and passionate extremes. By piling on details, sensations and images the Gothic style can seem exotic, extravagant and self-indulgent.

LANGUAGE DEVICE: ALLUSION

What is allusion?	Referring directly or indirectly to another topic or other books.
Example	Enfield describes the women around Hyde after he trampled the girl as being 'as wild as harpies' (p. 4). This is a reference to vengeful mythical creatures that were part bird, part woman.
Effect	This communicates that the women were furious and wanted revenge on Hyde.

An allusion or reference can be used as a quick, shorthand way of calling up an idea and its associations. As long as readers recognise the allusion, they understand a great deal from just a few words.

PROGRESS AND REVISION CHECK

SECTION ONE: CHECK YOUR KNOWLEDGE

1. Name two styles of story that have influenced the form of *The Strange Case of Dr Jekyll and Mr Hyde*.

2. Why does most of the action in *The Strange Case of Dr Mr Jekyll and Hyde* lack immediacy?

3. Which character uses the most imagery in their language?

4. Are the first eight chapters of *The Strange Case of Dr Jekyll and Mr Hyde* told by a first-person narrator or a third-person narrator?

5. To what tradition does the novella owe its preoccupation with horror, madness and intense emotion?

6. Why have Jekyll and Lanyon been friends for so long?

7. Why have Jekyll and Lanyon now fallen out?

8. What type of imagery stresses the inhumanity of Hyde?

9. Which character is most associated with the theme of the law?

10. Which aspect of London does Utterson glimpse through the fog on the journey to Hyde's lodgings?

> **TOP TIP** (A01)
>
> Answer these quick questions to test your basic knowledge of the form, structure and language of the novella.

SECTION TWO: CHECK YOUR UNDERSTANDING

Task: Consider how *The Strange Case of Dr Jekyll and Mr Hyde* relates to the detective novel. Think about:

● how its structure compares with that of a detective story

● which elements of the story show this.

> **TOP TIP** (A01)
>
> This task requires more thought and a slightly longer response. Try to write at least three to four paragraphs.

PROGRESS CHECK

GOOD PROGRESS

I can:

● explain how the writer uses form, structure and language to develop the action, show relationships and develop ideas. ☐

● use relevant quotations to support the points I make, and make reference to the effect of some language choices. ☐

EXCELLENT PROGRESS

I can:

● analyse in detail Stevenson's use of particular forms, structures and language techniques to convey ideas, create characters and evoke mood or setting. ☐

● select from a range of evidence, including apt quotations, to infer the effect of particular language choices, and to develop wider interpretations. ☐

UNDERSTANDING THE QUESTION

For your exam, you will be answering an extract-based question and/or a question on the whole of *The Strange Case of Dr Jekyll and Mr Hyde*. Check with your teacher to see what sort of question you are doing. Whatever the task, questions in exams will need decoding. This means highlighting and understanding the key words so that the answer you write is relevant.

BREAK DOWN THE QUESTION

Pick out the **key words** or **phrases**. For example:

Read the extract from Chapter 6 starting 'A week afterwards Dr Lanyon took to his bed' (p. 32) and ending 'the inmost corner of his private safe' (p. 33).

Question: What **role** does **secrecy** play in **this extract** and in *The Strange Case of Dr Jekyll and Mr Hyde* **as a whole**?

What does this tell you?

- Focus on **secrecy**, first working out which things are kept secret in the novella and the effect of keeping them secret.
- The word 'role' tells you that you should concentrate on the purpose and effect of secrecy in the novella.
- The phrases 'this extract' and 'as a whole' mean you need to **start** with the given **extract** and then **widen your discussion** to the rest of the novella, but sticking to the topic in both.

<table>
<tr><td>

TOP TIP   **A01**

You might be asked to 'refer closely to', which means picking out specific examples from the novella, or to focus on 'methods and techniques' which mean the 'things' Stevenson does, for example, the use of a particular language feature, an ironic comment on an event, etc.

</td></tr>
</table>

PLANNING YOUR ANSWER

It is vital that you generate ideas quickly, and plan your answer efficiently when you sit the exam. Stick to your plan and, with a watch at your side, tick off each part as you progress.

STAGE 1: GENERATE IDEAS QUICKLY

Very briefly **list your key ideas** based on the question you have **decoded**. For example:

In the **extract**:

- *Utterson locks himself in his business room so that he will not be observed or disturbed.*
- *The document (which is Lanyon's narrative) is in a sealed envelope and must remain secret until Jekyll dies or disappears; this unnerves Utterson and makes him curious.*
- *He respects Lanyon's wish and locks the document away, keeping the secret.*
- *As readers, we are keen to know what is in the document; it is frustrating and tantalising that Utterson does not read it. This helps to build suspense and hold our interest.*

In the **novella as a whole**:

- *Jekyll keeps his potion and the source of his distress secret, only eventually revealing it to Lanyon when he has no choice.*
- *Hyde has a secret life.*
- *Jekyll has uncovered forbidden knowledge that humans cannot bear knowing – it kills Lanyon as well as Jekyll.*
- *By keeping vital information hidden until the end, Stevenson builds suspense and mystery.*

STAGE 2: JOT DOWN USEFUL QUOTATIONS (OR KEY EVENTS)

For example, from the **extract**: 'the packet slept in the inmost corner of his private safe' (p. 33).

From **the novella as a whole**: 'I sometimes think if we knew all, we should be more glad to get away' (Lanyon, p. 31).

STAGE 3: PLAN FOR PARAGRAPHS

Use paragraphs to plan your answer. For example:

Paragraph	Point
Paragraph 1	**Introduce** the **argument** you wish to make: *Secrecy is an important aspect of the novella, both within in the action and in the way Stevenson tells the story, and our reaction as readers to it.*
Paragraph 2	Your first point: *In the extract, Utterson is faced with a document that probably tells Jekyll's secret and he has to decide whether to respect the wishes of Lanyon and Jekyll or give in to his curiosity. He decides to act honourably and keep the document locked away until Jekyll dies or disappears.*
Paragraph 3	Your second point: *Jekyll kept secret parts of his life that he was ashamed of. This meant that he was leading a double life, and finally led him to develop his potion.*
Paragraph 4	Your third point: *From the harmless secret of keeping his pleasures private, he has fallen into a far greater one – having to keep Hyde and his crimes secret. He cannot share this with his friends.*
Paragraph 5	Your fourth point: *There is a sense that Jekyll has come across 'forbidden' knowledge that must lead to his downfall and death. Lanyon, too, is unable to bear this forbidden knowledge and dies as a result of what he learns.*
Paragraph 6	Your fifth point: *Stevenson uses the secrets in the text to build mystery and suspense. We do not learn Jekyll's secret until the end – the whole novella turns on it and its being revealed to us.*
Conclusion	**Sum up** your argument: *Secrecy is central to the story and the way it is told. Besides Jekyll's greatest secret – the existence of Hyde and the potion – there are numerous other things kept secret, from the characters and from the reader.*

TOP TIP (A02)

When discussing Stevenson's language, make sure you refer to the techniques he uses, and, most importantly, the **effect** of those techniques. Don't just say: 'Stevenson uses extravagant imagery here', write 'Stevenson's use of imagery has the effect of ...'

RESPONDING TO WRITERS' EFFECTS

The two most important assessment objectives are **AO1** and **AO2**. They are about *what* writers do (the choices they make, and the effects these create), *what* your ideas are (your analysis and interpretation), and *how* you write about them (how well you explain your ideas).

ASSESSMENT OBJECTIVE 1

What does it say?	What does it mean?	Dos and dont's
Read, understand and respond to texts. Students should be able to: ● Maintain a critical style and develop an informed personal response ● Use textual references, including quotations, to support and illustrate interpretations	You must: ● Use some of the literary terms you have learned (correctly!) ● Write in a professional way (not a sloppy, chatty way) ● Show you have thought for yourself ● Back up your ideas with examples, including quotations	**Don't write:** *Lanyon gets cross and stroppy when Utterson asks him about Jekyll as he doesn't want to talk about him and gets pretty agitated, saying if he can't talk about anything else, 'then, in God's name, go, for I cannot bear it'.* **Do write:** *Lanyon is distressed and agitated when Utterson asks him about Jekyll. He refuses to talk about him, the extent of his anxiety clear in his plea to talk of something else or, 'in God's name, go, for I cannot bear it'.*

IMPROVING YOUR CRITICAL STYLE

Use a variety of words to show effects:

> **Stevenson** *suggests ..., conveys ..., implies ..., presents how ..., explores ..., demonstrates ..., describes how ..., shows how ...*.
>
> **I/we** (as readers) *infer ..., recognise ..., understand ..., question ..., see ..., are given ..., reflect ....*

For example, look at these two paragraphs. Note the difference in the quality of expression.

Student A:

Better to say how Stevenson 'depicts Hyde as' or 'shows Hyde as'

It is not Stevenson speaking to us

Too informal

Stevenson makes Hyde horrible and violent. He smashes into a small child and isn't even sorry – he just keeps going. This is the first time we see Hyde, and it makes us think he's going to be a bad character in the novella. Stevenson says Hyde 'trampled calmly' over the child, which is really nasty and makes us cringe. Everyone thinks Hyde is really horrid.

Style too informal and chatty

Better to say 'leads us to expect that' or 'suggests that'

Repetitive and vague

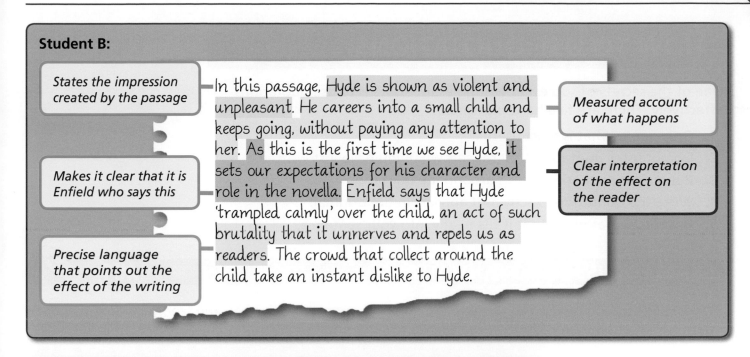

Student B:

States the impression created by the passage

Makes it clear that it is Enfield who says this

Precise language that points out the effect of the writing

In this passage, Hyde is shown as violent and unpleasant. He careers into a small child and keeps going, without paying any attention to her. As this is the first time we see Hyde, it sets our expectations for his character and role in the novella. Enfield says that Hyde 'trampled calmly' over the child, an act of such brutality that it unnerves and repels us as readers. The crowd that collect around the child take an instant dislike to Hyde.

Measured account of what happens

Clear interpretation of the effect on the reader

ASSESSMENT OBJECTIVE 2

What does it say?	What does it mean?	Dos and don'ts
Analyse the language, form and structure used by the writer to create meanings and effects, using relevant subject terminology where appropriate.	'Analyse' – comment **in detail** on **particular aspects** of the text or language. 'Language' – vocabulary, imagery, variety of sentences, dialogue/speech, etc. 'Form' – how the story is told (e.g. first-person narrative, letters, diaries, chapter by chapter). 'Structure' – the order in which events are revealed, or in which characters appear, or descriptions are presented. 'Create meaning' – what can we, as readers, infer from what the writer tells us? What is implied by particular descriptions, or events? 'Subject terminology' – words you should use when writing about novels, such as **character**, protagonist, **imagery**, **setting**, etc.	**Don't write:** *Stevenson uses lots of images here so I get a good sense of how Jekyll feels.* **Do write:** *Jekyll uses vivid imagery in his account of how he feels, to try to communicate the nature of feelings that are alien to everyone but him. He says Hyde is 'closer than an eye', and uses the metaphor 'caged in his flesh', both of which convey the sense the Hyde is a part of him that cannot be removed.*

THE THREE 'I'S

- The best analysis focuses on specific ideas, events or uses of language and thinks about what is **implied.**

- This means looking beyond the obvious and drawing **inferences**. Jekyll says that the faults he kept hidden were no more than a 'gaiety of disposition' (p. 57) and 'undignified' (p. 63), but that Hyde committed far worse crimes. These are not named, but from what we witness of Hyde – his trampling of the girl and murder of Carew – we assume they are terrible.

- From the inferences you make across the text as a whole, you can arrive at your own **interpretation** – a sense of the bigger picture, or a wider evaluation of a person, relationship or idea.

HOW TO USE QUOTATIONS

One of the secrets of success in writing exam essays is to use quotations **effectively**. There are five basic principles:

1. Only quote what is most useful.
2. Do not use a quotation that repeats what you have just written.
3. Put quotation marks, e.g. ' ', around the quotation.
4. Write the quotation exactly as it appears in the original.
5. Use the quotation so that it fits neatly into your sentence.

EXAM FOCUS: USING QUOTATIONS   (A01)

Quotations should be used to develop the line of thought in your essay and 'zoom in' on key details such as language choices. The example below shows a clear and effective way of doing this.

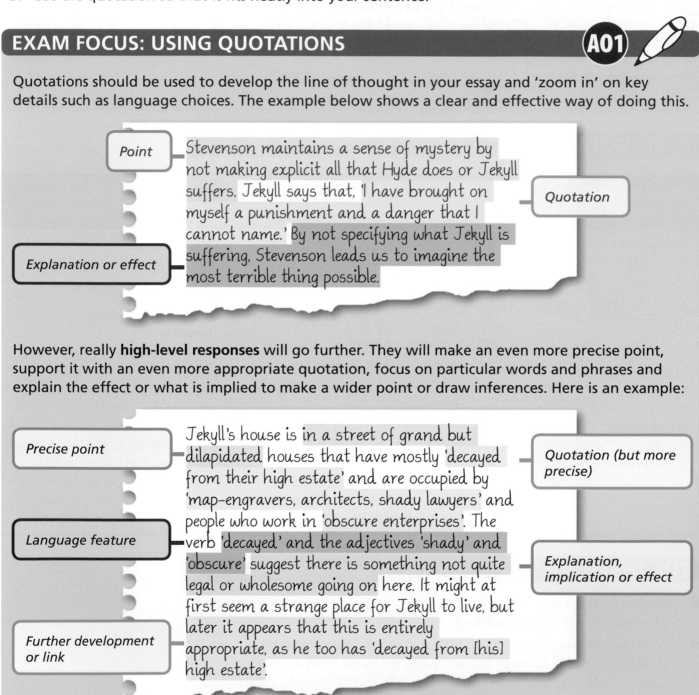

Point

Stevenson maintains a sense of mystery by not making explicit all that Hyde does or Jekyll suffers. Jekyll says that, 'I have brought on myself a punishment and a danger that I cannot name.' By not specifying what Jekyll is suffering, Stevenson leads us to imagine the most terrible thing possible.

Quotation

Explanation or effect

However, really **high-level responses** will go further. They will make an even more precise point, support it with an even more appropriate quotation, focus on particular words and phrases and explain the effect or what is implied to make a wider point or draw inferences. Here is an example:

Precise point

Jekyll's house is in a street of grand but dilapidated houses that have mostly 'decayed from their high estate' and are occupied by 'map-engravers, architects, shady lawyers' and people who work in 'obscure enterprises'. The verb 'decayed' and the adjectives 'shady' and 'obscure' suggest there is something not quite legal or wholesome going on here. It might at first seem a strange place for Jekyll to live, but later it appears that this is entirely appropriate, as he too has 'decayed from [his] high estate'.

Quotation (but more precise)

Language feature

Explanation, implication or effect

Further development or link

SPELLING, PUNCTUATION AND GRAMMAR

SPELLING

Remember to spell correctly the **author's** name, the names of all the **characters**, and the **names of places**.

It is a good idea to list some of the key spellings you know you sometimes get wrong *before* the exam starts. Then use it to check as you go along. Sometimes it is easy to make small errors as you write but if you have your key word list nearby you can check against it.

PUNCTUATION

Remember:

- Use **full stops and commas in sentences accurately to make clear points**. Don't write long, rambling sentences that don't make sense; equally, avoid using a lot of short repetitive ones. Write in a fluent way, using linking words and phrases, and use **inverted commas** for **quotations**.

Don't write:	Do write:
Lanyon and Jekyll were originally friends, they have fallen out because they disagree about what counts as science, Lanyon thinks Jekyll is too 'fanciful' to be a proper scientist, Jekyll thinks Lanyon is narrow-minded.	*Lanyon and Jekyll were originally friends, but they have fallen out because they disagree about what counts as science. Lanyon thinks Jekyll is too 'fanciful' to be a proper scientist, while Jekyll thinks Lanyon is narrow-minded.*

GRAMMAR

When you are writing about the text, make sure you:

- Use the present tense for discussing what the writer does.
- Use pronouns and references back to make your writing flow.

Don't write:	Do write:
Although Utterson was keen to help Jekyll with whatever problem was troubling Jekyll, Jekyll was unable to share his terrible secret with Utterson.	*Although Utterson **is** keen to help Jekyll with whatever problem **is** troubling **him**, Jekyll **is** unable to share his terrible secret with **him**.*

TOP TIP (A04)

Unless you are studying OCR, spelling, punctuation and grammar (AO4) won't be formally assessed in your exam on *Dr Jekyll and Mr Hyde*. However, it is still important to ensure that you write accurately and clearly, in order to get your points across to the examiner in the best possible way.

TOP TIP (A04)

Practise your spellings of key literary terms you might use when writing about the text such as: ironic, third-person narrator, simile, metaphor, imagery, protagonist, character, theme, interpolated narrative, etc.

TOP TIP (A04)

Improve your writing by varying the way your sentences begin. For example, *When Jekyll takes his potion, he feels extreme pain and nausea. When he feels he has changed, he goes to look in a mirror. When he sees himself, he is shocked* could instead be written as: *When Jekyll takes his potion, he feels extreme pain and nausea. He goes to look in a mirror because he feels he has changed, and he is shocked by what he sees.*

ANNOTATED SAMPLE ANSWERS

This section provides three sample responses, one at **mid level**, one at a **good level** and one at a **very high level**.

Question: Read from 'He sprang to it' **(Chapter 9, p. 54)** to 'you who have derided your superiors – behold!' **(p. 55).**

Discuss the interaction between Lanyon and Hyde in this extract. Write about:

- How it relates to the relationship between Lanyon and Jekyll/Hyde in the rest of the novella.
- The relevance of Lanyon not knowing who Hyde is.

SAMPLE ANSWER 1

A01 Sums up first impressions

Hyde has come to Lanyon's house to pick up the chemicals Lanyon has collected from Jekyll's laboratory. Jekyll doesn't know who Hyde is and he immediately dislikes him. This is the usual thought of people seeing Hyde for the first time. So at the start of the passage, Lanyon doesn't like Hyde and Hyde is desperate – he is frightened as he is grating his teeth and looking 'ghastly'.

A02 Notes language and gives simple account of what it implies

A02 Identifies effect of change of focus, informally expressed

Lanyon tells Hyde to 'Compose yourself', meaning to calm down. Hyde changes a bit as soon as he has the chemicals. Lanyon is interested in the chemicals and describes those for a paragraph, so we don't really see how Hyde is behaving or seeming then. When he starts talking again he has got cocky, and starts to be rude to Lanyon. He uses fancy language that is more like Jekyll's language. He seems to make it sound bad whatever Lanyon chooses: if he doesn't watch Hyde's transformation, he's missing out on something amazing, but if he does watch it's because of the 'greed of curiosity'. 'Greed' is a bad thing, so he makes it sound like Lanyon can't control himself.

A01 Language too informal

A02 Identifies style of language but not effect

A02 Identifies effect of word choice

Hyde warns Lanyon that what he sees next won't be good. It will 'blast' his sight, and will be so astonishing that even Satan would find it hard to believe. But Lanyon doesn't listen to the warning because he doesn't really believe Hyde. Hyde is pleased that Lanyon has decided to watch – he says 'It is well'. This is mean because it is going to be bad for Lanyon.

A01 Sums up state of relationship

A01 Use of correct term but repetitive

A01 Sums up this part of the essay

A01 Relevant quotation embedded

In the rest of the story, Jekyll and Lanyon are enemies. They used to be friends but they have fallen out and don't talk to each other any more. Lanyon has told Utterson that he regards Jekyll as dead. In this part, Hyde is rude to Lanyon, even though Lanyon has gone to get the chemicals he wanted. Hyde is really Jekyll's alter ego but Lanyon doesn't know that yet. Hyde is continuing Jekyll's fight with Lanyon, but Lanyon doesn't know that because he doesn't know who Hyde is. So the passage carries on the relationship between the two men in the rest of the story, except that Lanyon doesn't know it.

After this, Lanyon is horrified by seeing Hyde change into Jekyll and then hearing what Jekyll tells him (which he doesn't tell us). He says his life is 'shaken to its roots' and he will die soon. Effectively, Jekyll and Hyde have killed him by letting him see the transformation and then explaining it all. So they have beaten Jekyll's enemy. It's too hard a punishment just because Lanyon didn't agree with Jekyll over science. Because Hyde is so evil, though, he is willing to do this to prove that he (Jekyll) was right all along.

A01 Mistake in chronology – this happens after these events

A01 Accurate, but expressed in a confused way

A01 Attempt at personal interpretation

MID LEVEL

Comment
The essay raises some points that are relevant to the question, but shows a fairly basic understanding of the relationship between Lanyon and Jekyll/Hyde. The student tends to tell the story and drift away from the question. There is some use of quotation to support points, but there needs to be more detailed examination of language and its effects. There is no reference to context or the theme of science that lies at the heart of the relationship between Lanyon and Jekyll.

For a Good Level:
- Have a clear structure which answers the question through a logical sequence of points.
- Write in a more formal style.
- Make sure you understand the sequence of episodes in the plot.
- Include some mention of science, which is an important link between Lanyon and Jekyll/Hyde.
- Look more closely at the effects of the language Stevenson uses, with more quotations.

SAMPLE ANSWER 2

A01
Good point that Lanyon does not know who Hyde is, but nothing is made of it

This passage comes from Lanyon's account of his meeting with Hyde, when Hyde comes to pick up the chemicals to make his potion. Lanyon has not seen or met Hyde before, so he doesn't know who he is. This is their only meeting.

Lanyon finds Hyde horrifying when he meets him, like everyone else. Lanyon is a medical doctor and a gentleman, so he keeps this feeling to himself, except that he is rather abrupt with Hyde when he grabs at him. He does, though, give an account of his own physical response to Hyde's ugliness, which shows him being interested in a scientific way.

A01
Not relevant to the question

A02
Shows how language lets us know unstated feelings

A01
Notices effect of what is missed out

Lanyon is scared throughout this meeting. He has already prepared his gun and keeps it by him when he lets Hyde in. He says he is worried about Hyde when he grates his teeth and his face looks 'ghastly'. He is 'petrified' when Hyde sobs on seeing the chemicals he needs. Lanyon doesn't dwell on his own feelings, though. He goes on to describe the fizzing potion and then reports Hyde's speech and his own. He doesn't give much commentary on what happens so it's hard to know what he is thinking. Lanyon spends some time describing what happened to the potion. He also goes on to describe what happens to Hyde as he changes. Because Lanyon is a doctor and a scientist, he is interested in these scientific processes. He focuses on the parts he can understand in what he is seeing, the parts that look scientific. Victorian readers would have been interested in the science as there was great public concern about the many scientific advances going on at the time. Science is a significant context in Jekyll and Hyde, and this is the only part when we really see some science going on, so it's an important passage.

A03
Basic relation to contemporary context

A01
Identifies motivation, but expressed informally

Hyde is immediately quite aggressive to Lanyon. He taunts him by saying he would be wise not to watch, but suggesting he will be richer and wiser if he does watch. He is trying to make Lanyon watch the transformation, and he knows it will horrify him. This is mean, and it's probably not something that Jekyll would do himself because he has said that Lanyon is one of his 'oldest friends'. But Hyde is the evil alter ego of Jekyll and will enjoy Lanyon being distressed.

A01 Deduces hidden meaning from language used

A01 Relates passage to the wider text

A03 Contextual reference helps reveal character differences

Lanyon responds by not rising to the bait. He says he doesn't really believe Hyde, so he will stay and watch. This is what Hyde wants, and he then gloats over Lanyon, saying he has 'derided your superiors' – meaning Jekyll is superior to him. This refers to the argument between Lanyon and Jekyll in the rest of the novella. Lanyon is a normal type of doctor, who takes a very scientific view of things. Jekyll is interested in a different type of science, which he calls 'transcendental'. This is something Lanyon considers 'utter balderdash', and he even says that Jekyll is 'wrong in mind' for experimenting with it. The disagreement between them has led them to stop talking to each other, but in his note to Lanyon asking for his help with getting the potion he says they 'may have differed at times on scientific questions'. This makes it sound much less important, but Jekyll is trying to get Lanyon's help at this point. Even so, Lanyon does decide to help Jekyll and goes to get the drawer of chemicals, which suggests there is some bit of friendship left.

A01 Analysis of character's motivation

At the end of this passage, Lanyon is being defiant and saying he doesn't believe Hyde, but actually we've seen that he is scared throughout the meeting. And Hyde is being arrogant and saying that Lanyon will see something astonishing and will have to admit he was wrong. It looks like a continuation of the argument between Jekyll and Lanyon, but it will be more than that, as Lanyon is destroyed by what he sees. It's not even clear whether Jekyll knows or cares how much harm this does Lanyon, as later he says Lanyon's state 'perhaps affected me somewhat' but it was 'a drop in the sea to the abhorrence' with which he viewed the evening. But Lanyon says afterwards that his life was 'shaken to its roots' and he never recovered. So in this chapter, Lanyon is being good to Jekyll and doing what he asks, even though they are not friends any more, but Hyde is only being vengeful and mean once he has got what he wants.

A01 Relates relationship in wider text to this passage

A02 Good use of quotations to show state of mind

GOOD LEVEL

Comment
The answer tends to tell the story sometimes, but shows a good grasp of the relationship between Lanyon and Jekyll/Hyde, both here and in the wider novella. The response is reasonably well structured, though wording is sometimes a little informal. Some useful references to context, if occasionally undeveloped.

For a High Level:
- Give more detailed analysis of language and its effects.
- Relate the treatment of science more precisely to the contemporary context.
- Show the effect of what happens rather than just telling it.
- Structure the argument more logically.

SAMPLE ANSWER 3

A01 Points out important aspects of the passage

Lanyon's encounter with Hyde is the only meeting between the two, and contains Hyde's only long speech in the novella. It culminates in the revelation of the secret at the heart of the novella – that Hyde is Jekyll's alter ego. As such, this encounter is a crucial scene and the relationship between the main characters, Lanyon and Jekyll/Hyde, is clarified through it.

A01 Excellent account of the importance of the scene

A02 Interprets character's behaviour

A01 Explains relevance and effect

Lanyon, like others before him, is instantly repelled by Hyde. This is compounded by the anxiety and rudeness displayed by Hyde, who grabs desperately at him. Lanyon's language communicates his dislike; we too might wince at the idea of his teeth grating and his 'ghastly' face. In showing Lanyon clinically analysing his own response to Hyde, Stevenson reminds us of Lanyon's attitude to science, which is his point of difference with Jekyll/Hyde.

A02 Shows effect of language on the reader

A01 Personal interpretation of text

Once he has his potion, Hyde is more confident. His long speech to Lanyon is fluent and articulate. Hyde has the advantage of knowing who Lanyon is, but Lanyon does not know who Hyde is. Hyde becomes arrogant, disdainful and rude, even suggesting he (Hyde/Jekyll) is superior to Lanyon, who has 'derided [his] superiors'. Maybe this is how Jekyll secretly views Lanyon. The note asking for his help refers to Lanyon as one of Jekyll's 'oldest friends' and to their argument as differences of scientific opinion. It appears from Hyde's outburst here, though, that Jekyll/Hyde's real view is less generous.

A02 Shows understanding of language used to communicate character

A02 Relevant quotation fluently embedded

A03 Excellent explanation of contextual detail

When Hyde asks whether Lanyon wants to witness what will happen, Lanyon has no idea what he is being offered. Hyde presents the choice cleverly: he advises Lanyon to let him take the potion outside ('Will you be wise?'), but then challenges him to be brave and curious, making it hard for him to refuse. His extravagant promise of a 'new province of knowledge', a route to 'fame and power' and 'a prodigy to stagger the unbelief of Satan' appeal to Lanyon's scientific curiosity. The reference to Satan recalls Faust's deal with the Devil, exchanging his soul for knowledge, riches and power. This is what Hyde is offering,

A02 Shows how use of language works

A02 Sophisticated understanding of implications of language

and Lanyon would do well to refuse it. Hyde might be luring Lanyon to his doom on purpose, as Jekyll says that Hyde would drink 'pleasure with bestial avidity from any degree of torture to another'.

Lanyon responds by belittling the challenge – he has 'no very strong impression of belief' and is not going to admit to any fear. He does not pick up on the clues in Hyde's speech – the reference to 'our' profession (that which Lanyon shares with Jekyll), or the intimate knowledge Hyde has of Lanyon's scientific views.

A01 Awareness of subtleties in the text

A01 Describes established relationship between characters

A01 Good relation of passage to other parts of the novella

In the rest of the novella, Jekyll and Lanyon are presented as old professional friends who have different approaches to science. Lanyon's approach is very practical. It is demonstrated here in his attempt to give a precise, scientific account of all that happens – of how Hyde makes him feel, the mixing of the potion, and how Hyde changes. This is the approach Hyde (speaking for Jekyll) calls 'narrow and material'. Jekyll's interest is in 'transcendental' science, perhaps related to the new subject of psychology and the interest in the nature of humankind which Darwin's theory of evolution raised. Lanyon considers this approach 'fanciful' and 'unscientific balderdash'. Despite these differences, they are both curious, intelligent scientists in pursuit of knowledge.

A03 Reference to relevant contemporary science context

A01 Quotation embedded and well used

In repeating 'you who have …' and ending with the interjection 'behold!' Hyde's final speech adopts a theatrical air that is without warmth or gratitude but instead conveys a feeling of triumph – he will prove Jekyll/Hyde right, and Lanyon will have to believe him. Hyde defeats Lanyon and drags him down with him to his doom. The experiment has destroyed Jekyll, and now it will also destroy Lanyon. What in Jekyll's hands was a professional dispute has become in Hyde's hands a vindictive and dangerous show of strength.

A02 Detailed analysis of language and its effects

A01 Good closing sentence shows clear grasp of question

VERY HIGH LEVEL

Comment
This is a convincing essay that makes excellent use of evidence from the text outside the passage, and shows detailed understanding of how language is used to communicate information and create effects. It is very fluent, and expresses some original ideas and insights, relating several key ideas to complex contexts.

PRACTICE TASK

Write a full-length response to this exam-style question and then use the **Mark scheme** on page 88 to assess your own response.

> Read from: 'The steps drew swiftly nearer' (p. 12) to 'disappeared into the house' (p. 13). In this chapter, Utterson has been watching for Hyde when he finally sees him for the first time.
>
> How does Stevenson present Hyde in this extract and elsewhere in the novella?
>
> Write about:
>
> - how Stevenson presents Hyde in this extract
> - how he is presented in the rest of the novella

TOP TIP (A01)

You can use General skills section of the **Mark scheme** on page 88 to remind you of the key criteria you'll need to cover.

Remember:

- Plan quickly and efficiently by using key words from the question.
- Write equally about the extract and the rest of the novella.
- Focus on the techniques Stevenson uses and the effect on the reader.
- Support your ideas with relevant evidence, including quotations.

FURTHER QUESTIONS

1 In Chapter 4, Utterson accompanies Newcomen on a journey to Hyde's lodgings. Read from 'It was by this time about nine in the morning' (p. 22) to 'a man who was heir to a quarter of a million sterling' (p. 23).

How does Stevenson use setting to create an effect in this extract and in the rest of the novella?

2 Jekyll refers to what has happened to him as a 'shipwreck' (pp. 50, 58) yet Guest's verdict of his handwriting is that he is 'not mad' (p. 29). What is Jekyll's state by the end of the novella, and what does it suggest about humankind?

Consider:

- what Jekyll has done to himself and the effect it has had on his mind
- what the response of others (and Lanyon in particular) tells us about his discovery.

3 How does Robert Louis Stevenson use language to show character and to distinguish between characters?

Consider:

- how the language a character uses reveals or suits their personality
- how different characters express things differently.

LITERARY TERMS

alliteration	where the same sound is repeated in a stretch of language, usually at the beginnings of words
allusion	a reference, sometimes hidden in a word or phrase, which connects with another idea or text
alter ego	an alternative personality
character	a fictional person in a story
characterisation	creation of personality in a piece of writing through the way a person acts and speaks and how others act and speak towards them and about them
clause	group of words without a main verb
conjecture	an uncertain conclusion or inference drawn from incomplete information
connotation	connected idea or association that is brought to mind by a word, based on how the word is often used
euphemism	saying one thing, but meaning another, usually when the topic is embarrassing, upsetting or taboo. An example is saying 'passed away' instead of 'died'
first-person narrator	a voice telling a story from the first-person ('I') point of view, often used when the narrator is a character in the story
imagery	making pictures with words, using similes and/or metaphors
Gothic	a style of writing characterised by horror, extravagant settings and language, intense emotion and supernatural events
interjection	an exclamation in speech
interpolated narratives	short bits of story-telling inserted into a longer narrative, often through documents such as letters and diaries, or through one character telling another about an event or episode
irony	when a narrator or a character deliberately says one thing when they mean another, for humorous or sarcastic effect or to draw attention to an idea
literally	to mean exactly what the words say
literary device	a technique used by a writer, such as alliteration or imagery
metaphor	presenting one thing as though it were another, without making a comparison

narrative	a sequence of connected events that make a story
narrator	the voice telling a story
novella	a narrative that is longer than a short story but shorter than most novels
nuance	fine distinction of meaning, sense of feeling
objective correlative	using an object or state of external events or conditions to indicate something abstract, such as a character's state of mind or an idea
protagonist	the principal character in a work of literature
rhetorical question	a question that is asked with no expectation of an answer, often used to express surprise or disbelief or to show up the unexpected nature of things
rhythm	the pattern of sound made by strong and weak syllables in a line of text. It can force words to be read slowly or quickly, or create a distinctive beat
setting	the place and time in which a story takes place
simile	an image that compares one thing with another, using a word such as 'like' or 'as'
style	the combination of literary effects, including voice, imagery, sentence structure, use of narrators, rhythm, sound patterning and other devices that give a distinctive 'flavour' to a piece of writing
subject	the thing or person that a sentence is about
subordinate clause	a clause that is slotted into a sentence to add explanation or detail but that could be removed without disrupting the sentence
supposition	an assumption, or a belief held without good reason or evidence
theme	a subject or topic with which the story is concerned
third-person narrator	a narrator that refers to action happening to other characters and has no presence as 'I' in the story
verb	a word that shows action or state, such as 'eats', 'went', 'are', 'hopes'

CHECKPOINT ANSWERS, pages 8–32

1 As a lawyer, we can rely on him to tell the truth. He is shown to be dependable and thorough, and interested to get to the heart of matters.

2 He is a successful medical doctor, a long-time colleague of Jekyll's, but has an opposing view of science to that held by Jekyll and dismisses Jekyll's interests as unscientific.

3 He is a good friend, who wants to help Jekyll, but does not push Jekyll to the point of an argument. He is greatly valued by his friends.

4 Hyde gave him his address at the end of Chapter 2 when they met by the door.

5 As she sees an event that Utterson does not witness, Stevenson can use her to provide an account of the murder which could not otherwise be presented, as the story is told from Utterson's point of view.

6 He goes through the house and crosses the courtyard. The cabinet is up a flight of stairs from the laboratory.

7 He is a changed man – sick, anxious, fragile, shaken and aware that he is dying. His bad feeling towards Jekyll has greatly increased.

8 The look Utterson has seen cross Jekyll's face is so horrifying he knows something very terrible is happening to him.

9 He treats him as his social inferior, as a servant. Even though Poole is not Utterson's servant, Utterson feels able to question his behaviour, chastise him and tell him what to do. This is in keeping with the social structure of the time.

10 Jekyll has the cheval glass so that he can see his transformed self. It is tilted to the ceiling so that he cannot see himself on this final occasion.

11 He does not want to be seen, as he is wanted for the murder of Carew. If Jekyll's servants saw him, or if he was recognised by someone else, they would call the police.

12 He was already leading a double life in that he was a respectable public figure but went out secretly to pursue pleasures of which he was ashamed.

PROGRESS AND REVISION CHECK ANSWERS

PART TWO, pages 36–7

SECTION ONE: CHECK YOUR KNOWLEDGE

1 the door to Jekyll's laboratory

2 slowly accumulated them through exposure

3 £100

4 It provides for Hyde in case of not just Jekyll's death but his disappearance.

5 in order to counter the blackmail threat he imagines Jekyll faces

6 a maidservant

7 a broken walking stick

8 graphology (reading personality in handwriting)

9 a terrible shock

10 He is changing into Hyde.

11 He fears Jekyll has been killed.

12 an axe and a poker

13 The figure was too short to be Jekyll.

14 a broken and rusty key

15 There is a strong smell of kernels, indicating cyanide.

16 the red tincture and white crystals to make his potion

17 curiosity

18 He feels he has two conflicting aspects and wants to end his feeling of struggle.

19 The murder of Carew, as Hyde is now wanted by the police

20 the original salt only worked because it was impure, and he can't get more of it.

SECTION TWO: CHECK YOUR UNDERSTANDING

Task 1

The passage introduces the main aspects of Hyde that will be reinforced later in the novella.

- Physically, he is unusually short, but vigorous and strong – he walks quickly and easily tramples the girl: 'a little man who was stumping along eastward at a good walk' (p. 3).

- There is something odd about his appearance that can't quite be pinned down, but it is extremely repellent, causing Enfield and the doctor to want to kill him and the women present to attack him. 'He must be deformed somewhere; he gives a strong feeling of deformity, although I couldn't specify the point' (p. 6).

- He is exceptionally callous and unfeeling, showing no remorse for trampling the girl. He has 'a kind of black, sneering coolness' (p. 4).

- He is afraid of social ruin, responding to the threat of scandal by offering to buy off the family of the girl at any price the crowd names: '"No gentleman but wishes to avoid a scene," says he. "Name your figure"' (p. 4).

Hyde's odd behaviour and unpleasant appearance make Utterson curious.

- Hyde clearly has a connection with Jekyll (Utterson knows the door goes to Jekyll's property), and Jekyll is respectable: 'the very pink of the proprieties, celebrated too' (p. 5).

- Utterson can't understand why Jekyll would provide money to such an unpleasant person unless he were forced to do so.

- The questions in his mind prompt Utterson to find out more about Hyde.

Task 2

The cabinet is a civilised and pleasant space that has been violated and disordered.

- The violent account of breaking down the door prepares us for the violent disruption of Jekyll's space, as 'the red baize door leaped against the lock and hinges' (p. 44).

- The initial account of the cabinet is of an ordinary gentleman's sitting room, with the chair in a cosy place by a crackling fire, a kettle boiling and things set out for tea, and papers on the work table. It looks 'the most commonplace [room] that night in London' (p. 44).

- The calmness of the scene is destroyed by the 'body of a man sorely contorted and still twitching' on the floor and the strong smell of poison (p. 44). The discovery that it is Hyde is another jolt, as we might have expected Jekyll's body.

- Details bring the two aspects – civilised and disordered – into sharp focus by combining them in single objects: the mirror reflects both the 'rosy glow' of the fire and Poole's and Utterson's 'pale and fearful' faces (p. 46).

- Hyde has disrupted and vandalised the cabinet, just as he has disrupted and destroyed Jekyll's life.

- The disrupted cabinet encapsulates the dual aspect of Jekyll/Hyde, at once civilised and shocking.

- There is a devotional book on the table 'for which Jekyll had several times expressed a great esteem, annotated, in his own hand, with startling blasphemies' (p. 46). The affection for the book and the desecration of it show both aspects of the cabinet and of Jekyll/Hyde.

PART THREE, page 53

SECTION ONE: CHECK YOUR KNOWLEDGE

1. makes friends through long exposure and familiarity, and is then faithful
2. his hideous appearance and how they are repelled by him
3. He wants to keep his pleasures secret, and separate from his respectable life.
4. They have opposing views of science.
5. fear that Jekyll has in great danger or has been murdered
6. beautiful, elderly, innocent and kind
7. in case he turns into Hyde unexpectedly
8. he seems a reliable narrator
9. the way he uses language
10. his ambition

SECTION TWO: CHECK YOUR UNDERSTANDING

Plan

- Curiosity is an important driving force in *The Strange Case of Dr Jekyll and Mr Hyde.*
- Although Enfield says he is not curious, the three main characters are.
- Utterson's curiosity leads him to try to uncover who Hyde is and what is happening.
- Jekyll's scientific curiosity leads him to making his potion.
- Lanyon's curiosity leads him to watch Hyde take the potion.

Points to make

- Enfield says that 'You sit quietly on the top of a hill; and away the stone goes, starting others' (p. 5). This suggests that 'putting questions' (p. 5) is dangerous as it can lead to a cascade of events that lead in turn to unexpected and unpredictable terrible consequences.

- Utterson, as a lawyer, spends his life uncovering the truth. He has a rational and robust approach to finding out what is happening, but soon his curiosity in this case is fuelled by his concern for Jekyll and his imaginings of what might be going on: 'Hitherto it had touched him on the intellectual side alone; but now his imagination also was engaged or rather enslaved' (p. 10).

- Jekyll becomes obsessed with the question of whether humans have a dual nature and whether the parts can be separated. His scientific work and his philosophical questioning come together in pursuing this question: 'the temptation of a discovery so singular and profound, at last overcame the suggestions of alarm' (p. 59).

- Lanyon's scientific curiosity makes him take the chance to watch Hyde drink the potion, but what he witnesses drives him to despair as he cannot accept the answer it shows him. He says that Hyde 'struck in me what I can only describe as a disgustful curiosity' (p. 53).

PART FOUR, page 62

SECTION ONE: CHECK YOUR KNOWLEDGE

1. Lanyon and Jekyll
2. It has a respectable front part facing the street and the shady, battered door to the laboratory on a side street.
3. dealing with madness and horror; the supernatural
4. to make the setting sinister and spooky, and to make it possible for actions to be hidden
5. He trained in law at university.
6. Arthur Conan Doyle
7. Lanyon
8. Utterson's
9. allusion
10. Enfield, Lanyon and Jekyll

SECTION TWO: CHECK YOUR UNDERSTANDING

Plan

- Jekyll and Lanyon have different attitudes towards science and have fallen out over them.
- Present Lanyon's traditional view: science is a solid, practical, rational pursuit.
- Present Jekyll's view: science can deal with the 'transcendental', such as the relationship between body and mind or soul.
- Each is brought to disaster by sticking to their view.
- Science cannot be wholly defined by either approach.

Points to make

- Jekyll and Lanyon have very different views about what constitutes science and have fallen out over this. Jekyll says Lanyon has 'been bound to the most narrow and material views' and 'denied the virtue of transcendental medicine' (p. 55).
- Lanyon believes that science is a rational, practical subject in which everything can be explained by what we can detect with our senses. He puts his trust in observation, even giving a careful, medical account of the changes he sees overcome Hyde: 'he seemed to swell – his face became suddenly black and the features seemed to melt and alter' (p. 56).
- Jekyll believes science can deal with 'transcendental' phenomena. His interests are closer to what would now be considered psychology – the workings of the mind – than to physical medicine. But it is through practical science that he tries to separate the parts of himself: 'a side light began to shine upon the subject from the laboratory table' (p. 58).
- Both men are brought to death by their approach: Jekyll because he has unpicked himself and freed Hyde, and Lanyon because his mind can't deal with what he has seen. It appears that science is not enough to deal with the issues that Jekyll is interested in.

PART FIVE, page 69

SECTION ONE: CHECK YOUR KNOWLEDGE

1. detective novel and Gothic novel
2. It is narrated second-hand, after the event.
3. Jekyll
4. third-person narrator
5. Gothic
6. They are both medical doctors.
7. They disagree about the right approach to science.
8. imagery of Satan and animals
9. Utterson
10. poverty

SECTION TWO: CHECK YOUR UNDERSTANDING

Plan

- Explain what a traditional detective novel is – sets out a crime and follows the sequence of investigation to solve it.
- Does *The Strange Case of Dr Jekyll and Mr Hyde* set out a crime that needs solving? Not in a straightforward way: we know Hyde is responsible for the crimes committed.
- Does *The Strange Case of Dr Jekyll and Mr Hyde* follow the course of solving a crime? It shows Utterson trying to solve a mystery, but his detective work is not productive.
- The novella follows the rough pattern of setting up a mystery and solving it, but it is solved through the true nature of the action being revealed in documents, not through detective work.
- *The Strange Case of Dr Jekyll and Mr Hyde* owes something to the tradition of the detective novel but is not a detective novel itself.

Points to make

- A detective novel generally sets out a crime or mystery and then follows the course of the detectives solving it. In *The Strange Case of Dr Jekyll and Mr Hyde*, we know crimes have been committed by Hyde, but do not really know who he is – we know his name, but not his identity: 'his family could nowhere be traced; he had never been photographed' (p. 24).
- The nature of the crime is usually clear in a detective novel, but in *The Strange Case of Dr Jekyll and Mr Hyde* there is another 'crime' – Jekyll's use of his potion – which is not revealed until the end. Jekyll acknowledges he has done something bad, saying, 'If I am the chief of sinners' (p. 32).
- The crime or mystery is usually solved by careful work by a character investigating it. Utterson takes this role upon himself – '"If he be Mr Hyde," he had thought, "I shall be Mr Seek"' (p. 11) – but does not solve the mystery. The mystery is solved by the documents left by Lanyon and Jekyll.

MARK SCHEME

POINTS YOU COULD HAVE MADE

- Hyde's actions are brutal, callous and selfish.
- His physical appearance – short, with hairy, knotted hands and dusky skin; he seems to have something wrong with him – is suggested as the result of his being 'pure evil' (p. 61).
- Other characters are unaccountably repelled by his appearance; Enfield says 'I never saw a man I so disliked, and yet I scarce know why' (p. 6).
- Throughout the novella, characters are immediately repulsed by Hyde.
- His violence increases with the murder of Carew.
- Jekyll says Hyde's pleasures 'turn towards the monstrous' (p. 63); leaving the details to our imagination has more impact than giving gruesome details.
- He is surprisingly articulate in the narrative and the notes he writes – a clue that he is not what he seems.
- He lives in a low area, but his lodgings are tastefully furnished, a clue to his dual nature.

GENERAL SKILLS

Make a judgement about your level based on the points you made (above) and the skills you showed.

Level	Key elements	Writing skills	Tick your level
Very High	**Very well-structured answer which gives a rounded and convincing viewpoint.** You use very detailed analysis of the writer's methods and effects on the reader, using precise references which are fluently woven into what you say. You draw inferences, consider more than one perspective or angle, including the context where relevant, and make interpretations about the text as a whole.	You spell and punctuate with consistent accuracy, and use a very wide range of vocabulary and sentence structures to achieve effective control of meaning.	
Good to High	**A thoughtful, detailed response with well-chosen references.** At the top end, you address all aspects of the task in a clearly expressed way, and examine key aspects in detail. You are beginning to consider implications, explore alternative interpretations or ideas; at the top end, you do this fairly regularly and with some confidence.	You spell and punctuate with considerable accuracy, and use a considerable range of vocabulary and sentence structures to achieve general control of meaning.	
Mid	**A consistent response with clear understanding of the main ideas shown.** You use a range of references to support your ideas and your viewpoint is logical and easy to follow. Some evidence of commenting on writers' effects, though more needed.	You spell and punctuate with reasonable accuracy, and use a reasonable range of vocabulary and sentence structures.	
Lower	**Some relevant ideas but an inconsistent and rather simple response in places.** You show you have understood the task and you make some points to support what you say, but the evidence is not always well chosen. Your analysis is a bit basic and you do not comment in much detail on the writer's methods.	Your spelling and punctuation are inconsistent and your vocabulary and sentence structures are both limited. Some of these make your meaning unclear.	